Have Mercy!

THE SPRINGDALE SERIES III

*God's mercy shows up when we least expect it
…and need it most.*

A Novel by Award Winning Author

MARTHA B. HOOK

XULON ELITE

Xulon Press Elite
2301 Lucien Way #415
Maitland, FL 32751
407.339.4217
www.xulonpress.com

Unless otherwise indicated, Scripture quotations taken from the Holy Bible, New International Version (NIV). Copyright © 1973, 1978, 1984, 2011 by Biblica, Inc.™. Used by permission. All rights reserved.

Have Mercy! is a work of fiction. All people, places, and events are based on the late 1800s in American Southern culture and the author's imagination. No character or place in this story ever existed.

Printed in the United States of America.

ISBN-13: 978-1-54566-966-2

Dedicated
To those who have lost their childhood

"Lord, have mercy…."
Psalms 51:1

PROLOGUE

*T*he *Springdale Series* tells the post-Civil War story of Adam and Clarissa Norcutt and their family. Fans of award-winning *Glory Be!* will recall how a young widow and a British doctor become unusual friends as single parents. While struggling to provide for Baby Polly, Clarissa is hired to help Adam with his son, Nathan. An unlikely pair, the doctor and the widow fall in love and marry at Adam's restored plantation home. Recovery permeates this tale of two broken people who survive personal tragedy to begin a new life together at Fresh Meadows Farm.

In *Sakes Alive!,* second in *The Springdale Series*, the Norcutt family saga continues. Clarissa and Adam have twin sons, Warren and Wyatt. Leon Jonas, a homeless stable hand who barely survived his childhood living on the streets of Springdale, now works with Adam's horses. Also raising his half sister, Sunlight, Leon shares a shocking secret with Clarissa. When Leon is falsely accused of murdering his sweetheart, Rosalie, Dr. Adam and son, Nathan, step in to prevent his execution. A surprise visit from Josephine, Nathan's difficult British mother, assures Adam and Nathan that they're blessed to live across the Atlantic from her. Learning to forgive the fierce tentacles of long term abuse brings peace to the growing Norcutt family at Fresh Meadows Farm.

Now, welcome to ***Have Mercy!***, the final book of the Norcutt saga.

Part One

"I will deal with those who oppressed you
...at that time I will bring you home."
Zephaniah 3:19-20

CHAPTER 1

"The train's coming! Here we go! What a day!"
Shouts from the crowd waiting by the new railroad tracks filled the air around Springdale's first train depot. Everyone snuggled under their wraps and coats as a few snowflakes swirled in the wind.

A whistle sounded in the distance. Soon the ground shook as the locomotive drew near. Mayor Adam Norcutt and his wife, Clarissa, stood ready to greet this miracle of modern transportation.

"Can you believe this is really happening?" whispered Clarissa. "I'm so proud of you and your hard work to make this happen for our town."

"With all the naysayers, I thought we might never see this day," said Adam.

"And whoever thought my Dr. Adam Norcutt would be elected Mayor of Springdale, Kentucky?"

"Are these scissors sharp enough?"

"Adam, why are you so nervous? You're not doing surgery at your clinic. No one's life depends on this. Today you just need to cut a little ribbon after our first train is dedicated."

"Right, I can do that." Adam blew on his cold hands. "My friends in London won't believe I'm the Mayor of an American town."

"Well, you're the best man for this job. Just look at what you and your committee have accomplished."

"And, now we're waiting for the arrival of Springdale's first train."

"Thanks to your guidance, it's all worked out. But never forget, Adam, nothing is more important to our town than your clinic. Or you to my heart."

Adam's arm went around her waist and drew her closer.

"Pop, I can see the train now!" Nathan Norcutt, now as tall as his father, leaned over the railing of the platform. "Here we go!"

The crowd burst into cheers as the powerful black locomotive with its gleaming brass trim came around the bend. When it puffed to a stop alongside the new Springdale depot, several well-heeled railroad executives waved and exited a passenger car.

"Welcome to Springdale," said Adam as he shook their hands.

"Ladies and Gentlemen!" With the help of a large megaphone, Sheriff Olsen called the crowd to order. "Unlike our chilly weather today, we've planned a warm welcome to celebrate this important milestone for Springdale. As we join hands with their modern transportation company, we're pleased to have these distinguished executives with us today. Let's move forward together to meet the challenges and privileges of having this modern miracle of transportation right here in our own community."

The crowd cheered, and Sheriff Olsen motioned for Adam to come forward. "Now, please welcome our Mayor, Dr. Adam Norcutt. He's been a major force in bringing the railroad to our town. We are all in your debt, Dr. Norcutt."

"Thank you, Sheriff," said Adam as he took the megaphone. "Greetings to all as we celebrate this occasion. Many of you have worked long and hard for this day and we thank each one. Now, we've asked Father Joseph from our Catholic Church to bless this new facility. He will be followed by Rev. Steven Jackson of our Trinity Community Church who will offer a prayer of dedication."

The crowd quieted as Father Joseph came forward. His elaborate vestments sparkled in spite of the snowflakes. He reverently anointed and blessed the bumper of the train, then moved to anoint the entrance of the depot. When he was done, he offered a short prayer of blessing and crossed himself.

Next, Rev. Jackson prayed, "Almighty God, we thank you for bringing rail travel to Springdale. Please protect everyone involved, from those here at our new depot to those working along the line.

We also ask for the safety of those who will travel by rail to and from our city in the future. Amen."

He handed the megaphone to a railroad official who made a stiff official speech. "We're proud to assure Springdale of our support as we together undertake rail travel to this part of Kentucky. Now, make this official, Dr. Norcutt."

Adam waited for Sheriff Olsen to pull on a leather glove and grip a bottle of champagne. Together they walked to the wide red ribbon stretched across the shiny, new tracks. Accompanied by loud cheers, Adam cut the official ribbon and the sheriff broke the bottle of champagne on the bumper of the locomotive. At that moment, a new era began for Springdale.

Everyone moved inside to the warmth of the depot to visit with the dignitaries and have a serving of cake and champagne. Children crowded around for cookies and hot cider. With Polly Norcutt's help, Aunt Mag refilled platters with her homemade cake and cookies. Prudence Philips, who poured the champagne, clucked under her breath when people returned for a refill.

"Just who do you think is paying for all these bubbles of the devil?"

Finally, Aunt Mag took over Prudence's job, "Miss Pru, why don't you hand out cookies to the children? And try to smile, if you can."

As the festivities wound down, Leon Jonas, the trusted horseman in charge of the valuable horses for sale at Fresh Meadows Farm, approached Adam.

"What's up, Leon?" asked Adam.

"After that next sale in Lexington, what if we ship your new horses back to Fresh Meadows by rail? Travelling home by boxcar will only take a few hours, but that trip overland takes us two full days. And it's hard on the horses. Why not give it a try?"

"I hadn't thought of that possibility, Leon. Let's talk about it later. We need those new horses, the sooner the better."

Exhausted from the excitement of the day, Clarissa chatted with Adam before they fell asleep that evening. "Was Leon serious about shipping those horses home by rail?"

"I think he was," said Adam through a big yawn. "I'll give it some thought, but I like the idea. By the way, this time I'm sending him to the Lexington sale on his own. He's gone with me often enough to know what to do."

"Is he ready for that much responsibility? He can barely read or write."

"But he's the best when it comes to horses. He'll be fine."

"Then he must put on a better appearance. He can't represent Fresh Meadows Farm in his worn out work clothes."

"What if I send him to that new haberdasher at The Mercantile? That gentleman can outfit him for the Lexington sale. Nathan can go along to put everything on our account."

Nothing but silence came from the other side of the bed.

"So, you must agree with my idea?"

CHAPTER 2

*S*unlight rubbed her eyes against the early morning sunlight. Leon Jonas, her half brother, who was raising her as his daughter, dressed her and carried her into the warm Fresh Meadows kitchen for breakfast. He settled her in the battered highchair the Norcutt twins, Warren and Wyatt, no longer used.

Magnolia, who was born a slave on the original farm, baked fresh biscuits every morning. She sang as she greeted everyone coming into the huge plantation kitchen.

"Morning, Sunny. You and yo' Papa ready for some warm breakfast to start your day?"

"Yes, please," said Sunny as she carefully broke off pieces of the fresh biscuits to feed to the waiting farm dogs.

Willy, Magnolia's husband and Adam's farm manager, argued with Leon about who would muck out the stables after breakfast.

"Leon," said Magnolia. "Move yourself outside so's I won't have to listen to you and my Willy carry on. And take these dogs with you. They don't b'long in my kitchen eating biscuits."

"But it's cold out yonder," said Willy.

"Shoo!" She handed them a platter of biscuits and big bowls of hot grits as they left.

Nathan came out to join the men at the table under trees behind the kitchen. He shivered and helped himself to several of their biscuits.

"Miss Maggie," hollered Willy. "Could you bring Master Nathan some breakfast before he eats all ours? And we needs mo' hot coffee."

"All right!" Magnolia loved it when they fought over her cooking and wanted more.

Nathan leaned closer to Leon to whisper some news.

"…what?" Leon choked on his grits.

"You heard me. Pop is sending us to town. If you're representing him at that next horse sale, he wants you to clean up and get some new clothes."

"I'm already clean. I just washed up. Anyway, what's the matter with my clothes? I'll wear what I've always worn. He's never complained before."

"Calm down, Leon. Here's the problem. You look like you work in a barn. But if you're his buyer for Fresh Meadows in Lexington, you'd better spiff it up." He flipped the well-worn collar of Leon's shirt. "You'll be examining horses and making bids. He wants you dressed for the job. Pop is right about this."

"So, you agree with him?"

"Yes, so finish your grits and let's go. We still have work to do when we get back."

"I have to do this?"

"Right. And he's paying the bill, so no excuses."

The men walked toward their horses, but Leon still balked.

"No matter who pays for them, I don't need any fancy clothes. When I need something, I'll order it from your mother's catalogs or ask Aunt Mag to sew for me. She makes a better shirt than those silly women at your mother's boooooteeek."

"Leon, it's the 'Ladies' Fashion Boutique,' the shop where all those sweet girls like for you to come in with Sunny. You still don't understand, do you? Pop is making you his buyer. He's sending you alone to this sale. So, let's outfit you with the clothes to fit your new job."

"Wait a minute?" Leon hesitated. "This is a new job? For me?"

"Exactly!" He cuffed Leon on the back of his neck.

"Why didn't you tell me in the first place? I hadn't thought of it that way."

"Right, now let's go before you start arguing with me again."

The men mounted up for the ride into town, but before they left, Polly ran after them.

"Nathan, hold up!"

"No, Sis, you can't come with us."

"That's not it," she said, all out of breath. "I have a request for Leon."

"What's that?" Leon asked. "Chocolates? Ribbons?"

"No, will you do something else while you're in town?" She smiled at Leon and winked.

"And I won't like what you have in mind? Right?"

"Most probably not."

"So tell me, Miss Polly. Get it over with."

"While you're in town, stop at the barber. Get a decent haircut to go with your new clothes. And get a shave."

"Don't even think about that, Miss Polly."

"Just do it for me, Leon," she pouted. "Trust me, with new clothes and a trip to the barber, those Lexington ladies will notice. Make him do it, Nathan."

"Can't you control your sister, Nathan?"

"Sorry, I agree. I think Sis is right."

Leon rolled his eyes and took off at a fast pace on Miner Boy.

"I'll cut your hair if you don't go to the barber," she shouted. "And some chocolates would be nice. Get Nathan to pay for them."

Leon waved, but didn't look back.

CHAPTER 3

*T*he stock pens in the Lexington rail yard slowly emptied as waiting boxcars were loaded. Leon's newly purchased horses now kicked at their confinement in a boxcar on a side track. Other cars full of animals and products waited to be hitched to the scheduled locomotive bound for Springdale.

Excited passengers checked their tickets. Friends gathered to wish them "*Bon Voyage*." Still fascinated by new locomotives, several spectators gathered to watch for the train's arrival. Ladies waited under their warm shawls and fur muffs, while men pulled their overcoats closer. Brave youngsters set out new pennies on the tracks.

After no sign of the train, the depot manager announced, "Unfortunately, there will be a delay due to an accident several miles outside of Springdale. I have no idea how long the wait will be. I apologize for this unavoidable delay."

Leon Jonas, still flushed with his success at the Lexington auction, slapped his thigh with his new wide-brimmed hat. That Dr. Norcutt's expensive horses would have to wait in a crowded boxcar for a prolonged time did not make him happy. As he tried to calm the horses, he wondered if they had made the right decision to ship the horses to Fresh Meadows Farm by rail.

"Too late now," he muttered.

The day slipped away as did the curious onlookers. Disappointed children retrieved their pennies from the tracks. Ticket holders moved inside the depot out of the afternoon chill.

When the manager announced that the train was delayed until the next morning, Leon unloaded the doctor's horses into a holding pen. Exhausted and frustrated, he needed to find some food for his horses and supper for himself.

"You need some 'hep with them hungry horses?" a local farmer asked.

"I suppose so. It never occurred to me that we'd be stranded here."

"If you want, I'll feed and water 'em."

"I'd welcome your help. Let me know your tab."

Shivering in the cold wind, Leon walked across the road to the local saloon for some supper. After eating and fending off several flirtatious women, he returned to the depot.

Disgusted travelers sat around the waiting room in various stages of frustration. Resigned to the long night ahead, he settled down on a bare wooden bench, put his valise behind his back for safe-keeping, and pulled his hat over his eyes. Stretching his long legs out in front of him, he covered himself with his rain slicker and tried to stay warm. Even though his horses had calmed down a bit after they were fed, he couldn't shut off his concern for them. He also knew Dr. Norcutt would be fretting over this puzzling delay of the train carrying his new horses.

And why did that large man beside him snore like the anticipated locomotive? And why did that pitiful lady sitting across from him keep crying?

He never slept a wink.

When the post master opened his office in the depot, Leon smoothed his hair and stepped up to the window to send a wire to Dr. Norcutt about the delay. The postmaster hesitated to do business with him. Even with his new clothes and trip to the barber, Leon's high cheekbones and jet black eyes identified him with his Shawnee heritage.

"Look, Mister," said Leon. "My money is as good as yours. Just send the wire, if you please." With little patience left, he shoved the correct payment into the brass cup under the window. After another suspicious glance at Leon, the post master recounted the money before sending the wire.

Next, Leon went out to tend the horses in the station paddock. The helpful local farmer, waiting for his fee, agreed to feed and water the horses once more.

After he applied some ointment to a scrape on a gelding's leg, Leon headed once again to the local saloon. The cook, in sad shape from the past night's revelry, had to be prodded awake. Leon ordered some breakfast and a sandwich for later in the day. The women from the evening before never appeared. When he returned to the depot, he stopped to get a shoe shine at a stall just inside the entrance. He wanted to take care of his new boots, the nicest he'd ever owned.

The tiny lady who kept him awake during the night still huddled behind her shawl, sobbing. Without warning, she began ranting, maybe praying, in a strange language. A small man, nattily dressed in a rumpled black business suit with a black felt hat perched on his head, came over. He kept arguing with her in her language. The little man hurried over to the saloon, talked to the proprietor who leaned against the doorway, but came back empty handed.

Leon wondered why the man never offered the poor woman anything to eat or drink. Finally, he walked over to her. When she noticed the toes of his freshly polished boots, she looked up in fear.

"Miss, please. Have this." He handed her half of his sandwich.

She whispered, "Danke," and took Leon's sandwich. As he turned away, she grabbed his sleeve with a trembling hand. "Wasser, bitte?"

When Leon looked puzzled, she acted out her request with hand motions. He turned on his heel and returned with a granite cup of water begged from the post master. As she devoured Leon's provisions, she kept glancing at the man in the black suit. When Leon offered her a wrapped chocolate he'd bought for Sunny, her tear-stained face lit up with thanks.

He puzzled about this disheveled young lady, but with the language barrier he knew he could never understand her. The only solution was to talk to the man in the black suit.

"She's a mail order bride from Germany. What's it to you?"

"Look, I listened to her cry all night. She's rather upset about something."

"Wrong, Mister...she's very upset. The sorry excuse of a man who was supposed to marry her hasn't shown up."

"So, you'll take her back to Germany?"

"Nope! Got me a contract right here." He pulled a German document out of his vest pocket. "Her father sold her to the mail order company I work for. She can't go back to Germany."

"What? Her father sold her? I never heard of such a thing. Why would a parent do that?"

"When poor folks have too many mouths to feed, they get desperate. After this farmer's wife died, this girl was no help to him in the fields. He'd never wanted a girl anyway, especially one who can't cook and reads her Bible all the time. When my company came through looking for young ladies to marry husbands in America, he sold her. Got me a nice price, too."

"So, this is a business?"

"Sure is. I bring these brides over to America for their intendeds. I'm delivering this one to some farmer." He tipped his black hat with a superior air and shrugged. "He doesn't know she's another farmer's reject."

"Surely he'll show up, won't he? A mail order bride can't be cheap."

"He's already paid his bill in advance, but he ain't coming. We've waited for him for two days. If he doesn't claim her by the time this train leaves for Springdale, I have my orders what to do. It's all in writing in this here contract."

"So, what'll happen?"

"After 48 hours, I'm obliged to take her to that saloon." He pointed across the street.

"She'll work there as a cook or something?"

"Or something! Right about that, Mister!" The man scoffed at Leon's ignorance. "She'll be available to the men who frequent the saloon at night whenever they need—entertainment." He raised a knowing eyebrow.

"Wait! You'll leave her in that filthy saloon to become a prostitute?"

"Look, mister, this is a business, pure and simple. No marriage, she goes across the street. I got it all in a contract."

Without hesitation, Leon said, "Not this time."

"You want to marry her?"

"No, but I'll find her a decent home."

"Look, I appreciate your concern, but my contract says that without a marriage, she goes across the street. Look over yonder, you can see them saloon ladies already waiting for her."

"But this is no way to treat a helpless young girl."

"Well, good for you." The escort placed his hand over his heart in mock sympathy. "Look, the man who owns the saloon will have my hide if I don't abide by this contract. We work for the same company."

"But she's so young. How old is she anyway?"

"Because of our company's regulations, her father says she is 18. But I wager she's a lot younger. Anyway, who cares?"

Leon walked to the window and saw several bawdy women yawning and waving red scarves as they called out to welcome their new arrival. His stomach churned.

"Can't you break your contract if I cover your loss? She doesn't look like that sort." He motioned toward the saloon.

"Sorry, I'm a man of my word. Anyway, I already got my money."

The station master blew his whistle and shouted. "The train arrives in Lexington in 15 minutes. Immediate departure for Springdale."

CHAPTER 4

Afraid he might miss the train bound for Springdale, Leon rushed out to re-load Dr. Norcutt's geldings into their boxcar. But his mind would not let go of this girl trapped in such a horrible situation. How could a father sell a child? The rest of her life would be a nightmare at that saloon. She could run away, but how would she survive on her own?

Leon had not forgotten the business his Shawnee mother, Blue Lark, ran by necessity…and the obnoxious miners who came to visit her in their Minetown shack. They would shove him outside into the cold mountain air where he would shiver and try to sleep until Blue Lark pulled him back inside. When she could no longer feed him, he left their home and followed the steep path down to Springdale.

He remembered what it felt like to be a homeless youngster. With no home, he'd struggled to survive on the streets and alleys. He earned what he could by running errands and grooming horses. He would never forget the kindness of the owner of the Springdale Stables who let him sleep in the barn on cold nights nor the hotel proprietor who gave him leftover food.

"Lord, have mercy! What can I do for this girl? Surely, there's something?" In his next breath, he swallowed hard and asked, "Lord, really? I guess I could…."

While the locomotive backed into the switching yard to hitch up to the loaded boxcars, he ran back into the depot where the unscrupulous escort shoved the screaming girl toward the exit.

"Hold up!" Leon called across the waiting room.

"Mister, no more talk. The train is leaving and this girl's prom-ised has reneged on his contract. She goes across the street unless that farmer from Springdale shows up for her."

"What?" Leon's eyes widened. "Wait! A farmer from Springdale?"

"Someone named Featherson. Owns a big farm north of town."

Leon grabbed the contract to be sure Jacob Featherson's name was on it.

"Listen, this man died two weeks ago in a farm accident. He was a good man and a friend of mine. I helped dig his grave next to his wife who died in childbirth years ago. No one in Springdale knows he was expecting a mail order bride from Germany."

"So, he's dead? That's why he's a no-show? Well, guess he's got himself a good excuse, don't he?" He winked at Leon.

The girl's eyes filled with dismay as the man explained to her what had happened to her Farmer Featherson. With his tobacco stained finger, he pointed to the contract, then shoved her again toward her future at the saloon.

Leon lowered his voice and said, "Wait! I could marry her and not tell anyone we're married. That way, you'll fulfill your contract."

"You crazy? Why would you do that? Don't you want your own bride?"

"There aren't any available women in Springdale. Certainly none that will marry a part Shawnee man."

"But don't you want husbandly privileges with this girl if you marry her?"

"Look, mister, I'll marry this poor soul so she won't have to face life in that saloon. That's it, take it or leave it."

"I'll see what this little lady thinks of your offer."

He sat down with the girl and explained Leon's proposal. She stared long and hard at Leon, then asked several questions which the man translated.

"She wants to know, if you are one of them American Indians? If you are, will she have to live in a teepee?"

Showing his brilliant smile, Leon leaned back and laughed.

"Tell her my mother was Blue Lark, a Shawnee princess. My father was a white man who died when I was a little boy. Put her at ease, I've never seen a teepee near our town." He waited a moment for the man to translate his comments. "Look, tell her I'm perfectly safe. I work on a horse farm owned by a doctor. His wife runs a dress shop. They have four children. I live there with my daughter. This lady will have her own place to live."

The abandoned bride listened as the man translated Leon's unusual proposal. She thought quietly, muttered some prayers, and agreed to do it. But only if they lived in separate quarters and she would be safe.

"Of course," said Leon. "I can promise her that."

"I guess you got yourself a bride, mister."

"Sir, I don't have rings or a preacher."

"I got that all taken care of. You just have to sign some papers."

The man pulled a rusty pen staff and small bottle of ink from his valise. He spread out two copies of a marriage document for the bride and groom to sign.

"So...what's your name, ma'am?" asked Leon as he tried to decipher his bride's signature on the contract. After the escort translated his question, she turned pale blue, tear-filled eyes to him. "Gisela Schroeder."

The conductor blew his whistle and shouted, "Train leaves in five minutes."

"Need us a couple of witnesses, Mr. Jonas. Hurry!" said the man in black.

Leon found the man who had snored through the night before. "Could you and your wife come with me for a moment?" With no time to explain what was happening, Leon urged them over to where Gisela waited.

"Gotta be quick." The marriage broker held the right hands of the bride and groom together on top of a worn German-English dictionary. "You two want to be married?" he asked in both languages.

Leon and Gisela looked at each other with blank stares and nodded.

"Then you're man and wife. God bless you. Here's your rings. You may kiss the bride."

Leon slipped the rings into his pocket, but the preacher objected.

"Mister, I gotta see those rings on your fingers when you board that train."

Leon put the ring on his left hand and slid Gisela's onto hers. She stared at it a moment before she looked up at him. He struggled with what to say next.

"Gisela, I'm not ready for a kiss." When the broker translated his comment, Leon noticed she almost smiled.

After the bewildered best man and matron of honor signed as witnesses on the copies of the marriage document, Leon blew on the drying ink and slid their copy into his valise.

"Mr. Jonas, I'll file your marriage document here at the courthouse before I leave," said the broker. In German he continued, "Mrs. Jonas, here's your German passport. Don't lose it. Someday get it changed with your new name."

"You're gonna need this." He slapped his tattered German-English dictionary onto Leon's calloused palm. "By the way, she can read a little."

The cobbled together wedding party rushed out as the conductor waved his green lantern toward the engineer. The locomotive's mournful whistle performed the only recessional that accompanied the newlyweds down the aisle of the train and into their secret future.

CHAPTER 5

After Leon found seats for Gisela and himself, he stowed their luggage in the overhead racks. With her permission, he removed Gisela's ring and put it along with his in the outside pocket of his valise. When they were settled and the train picked up speed, he told her he needed to go check on his horses. But she grabbed his hand in fear.

"Trust me, young lady, I'll come back. I promised to help you out of this predicament. A promise is a promise."

After he left his new hat in her lap as a guarantee, she slid down in the seat and pulled her shawl around her shoulders. He muttered as he worked his way through the passenger car back to his horses.

"Lord, what have I done? The only word of German I know is this poor girl's name. I think it's 'Griselda' or something like that. God in heaven, why did I do this? But I just couldn't leave her in that filthy saloon…she's so young and afraid. She must also be sad about losing her promised life in America. I pray the Norcutts will agree with what I've done. If not, help me find her another safe place." As an afterthought, he added, "Lord, I'm sure of one thing… Blue Lark is smiling today."

When he returned to his seat, Gisela still wept. The little tan cap she wore over her blond braid tilted, but Leon caught it before it slid onto the dirty floor.

"Here, Gisela, you almost dropped this." At the sound of his attempt to say her name she straightened up. When she reached for the cap, she whispered, "Danke."

Remembering his struggles to learn English when he left his Shawnee home, he looked in the little dictionary for German words.

He did the best he could with a pencil stub and a scrap of paper he dug from his valise.

The first word he wrote down was SAFE. "Sicher," he pointed to himself. She nodded that she understood.

When he found the German word for FARM, she tried to explain something about herself and a FARM. He went on to the word for WORK and pointed to himself. Then he wrote HORSES and pointed in the direction of his boxcar full of horses. When Gisela frowned, he decided to show her the horses.

He held out his hand. "Let's go see HORSE."

She held back her hand until he pointed again to the word SAFE. When they reached the boxcar and she admired the beautiful horses, he said, "HORSE, all go with me to FARM."

"HORSE," she repeated as she rubbed the nose of the nearest, a black gelding. When Leon handed her a curry brush, she began brushing the horse's tangled mane. He had no way of knowing that she had never seen such beautiful horses. The ones on her poor family's farm pulled plows and heavy wagons. Invaluable to their farm, they were nothing like Dr. Norcutt's expensive new stock.

As he watched her, Leon's thoughts turned toward his friend in heaven. "Jacob, I think she'd have been a good farm wife. Sorry you died before you met her. Well, now she's my bride, but don't tell on us."

They returned to their seats as the conductor came through taking tickets and selling refreshments. Leon handed over his ticket and paid Gisela's fare. Next, he bought coffee for them, but when he asked Gisela to choose a pastry, she hesitated. When Leon said "SAFE" and she reached for the largest pastry, he realized she probably needed more food.

"Give her two of those and more coffee," he said to the conductor.

Surprised by his generosity, Gisela whispered, over and over, "Vielen Dank."

When he wrote THANK YOU on the scrap of paper, she tried to repeat it…her first attempt to communicate in English.

As the overdue train rushed through the countryside, Leon pointed out familiar things and underlined their German words in the dictionary. When they were a short distance from Springdale, he had no choice but to prepare her for the people who would greet them. Unfortunately, he had no way to warn them that a stray German girl would arrive along the new horses.

As Leon wrote down names for her, he told her, "All SAFE." She nodded that she understood.

DR. and MRS. NORCUTT own FARM. He's also our DOCTOR.

NATHAN, son.

POLLY, daughter.

WYATT and WARREN, twin sons. He held up two fingers.

SUNNY, he pointed to himself, "My daughter." Gisela looked puzzled, but he knew she'd never understand why he was raising his half-sister. He moved on to others at Fresh Meadows.

WILLY, helps with HORSES. MAGNOLIA, his wife, is our COOK. Both NEGROES.

Gisela pointed to the word "Negroes." He showed her the word for "black," rubbed his skin and said, "schwarz." Her eyes registered fear.

"Schwarz but SAFE."

When she looked up a word and pointed to it, "Der Besitzer," he realized she must think Dr. Norcutt owned Willy and Magnolia.

"No, all slaves free now. No one owns slaves in America now. All SAFE." She seemed satisfied with his explanation, so he went on.

MARCUS, farmer. PLESSIE, his wife, does ironing and watches Norcutt twins.

"All in Springdale." He pointed to the name of their destination on their tickets. "All SAFE."

She patted the names on the list and repeated, "Alle sicher." When he gave her the scribbled list, she slid it into the pocket of her apron, one worn and soiled from her journey across the Atlantic.

"Dear God," whispered Leon. "I had no time to wire ahead about this girl. I'm unprepared for her myself. Help us provide some security for her after all she's been through. Sold by your father? Almost a prostitute?" Wiping his brow with his bandana in frustration, Leon rested his elbows on his knees and prayed aloud.

"Heavenly Father, I pray that all at Fresh Meadows will understand the dilemma I faced when I saw those whores calling out for this young girl. Being sold as a mail order bride was bad enough. And I also pray that Sunny will take to Gisela."

He looked over at Gisela and said "Amen." Puzzled, she hesitated but said, "Amen."

He pulled the rings and the marriage document half way out of his valise and put his finger to his lips. "Big Secret! Don't tell. SHHHH!"

She touched her empty ring finger in agreement, "SHHHHH! Sicher." She pointed to him, "Name?"

"My name?" he asked and pointed to himself. When she nodded, he said, "Leon...Leon Jonas."

"Dankeschoen, Herr Leon," she said. "Vielen Dank."

"So, how do I say your name?" He pointed to her name in her passport: Gisela Schroder. "Gizella?"

Shaking her head, she corrected him, "Geessela."

After several tries, he said it in a way she approved. "G-eee-sell-ah."

"Gut."

CHAPTER 6

The train whistled and slowed for its arrival into Springdale. As the newly-weds stood on the exit platform of the passenger car, Leon tried with hand signals to explain the situation to his secret companion.

"You wait here. I must greet everyone and unload the horses."

Gisela watched as Leon was warmly welcomed by his Fresh Meadows family. She took out his scribbled list and tried to put names with the faces she saw. She easily identified Willy and Magnolia. Was Sunny the little girl in Magnolia's arms?

Leon sent Willy and Nathan to the boxcar to unload the horses. Dr. Adam went with them to inspect his new acquisitions. The twins ran past their father, but he grabbed their hands and cautioned them to be careful around the nervous, new horses.

"Papa!" Sunny squealed. When Magnolia put her down, she scampered to Leon. He picked her up, kissed her cheek and twirled her around.

"Gisela...." He reached with his free hand to help his bride down the steep steps of the passenger car. Silence settled over the greeting party. Questions without answers filled the air.

"Is this young lady with you, Leon?" whispered Clarissa.

"Sort of, Miss Clarissa. She's Gisela, Jacob Featherson's mail order bride from Germany. I found her in the depot in Lexington where she'd been waiting for him for two days." He silently thanked God for giving him the succinct answer he needed without lying. "She doesn't speak English."

"Sweet Jesus! That po' soul," said Magnolia.

"I'll tell everyone more about her in a minute," said Leon. "I can't remember her last name much less say it. She seems very sweet and she's plenty scared. Now that she knows she's safe, she's quit crying."

Clarissa stared at Leon. Her hazel eyes fired with gold as she asked, "What on earth?"

Acknowledging the dilemma he'd created, he shrugged. After the men finished tying up the new horses, they came over to see why a tiny travel-worn girl stood inside the circle of Fresh Meadows women. All stared, mesmerized.

"Gentlemen," said Leon. "I'd like you to meet Gisela from Germany. She waited at the station when our train for Springdale was delayed overnight. I couldn't sleep last night for her crying. When I asked the gentleman escorting her why she was so upset, he told me she was a mail order bride, but the groom who'd paid for her hadn't claimed her."

"Now ain't that a shame," said Willy.

"Willy, this story only gets worse. When the marriage broker mentioned that she was waiting for a farmer from Springdale, I found out she was Jacob Featherson's mail order bride."

"Come on, Leon," said Adam. "Jacob would've told us if he'd ordered a bride from Germany. Of all the crazy ideas! To order a wife through the mail? Sight unseen from Germany? Doesn't sound like something Jacob would do."

"I agree. But I guess he had that bad accident before he gathered up enough nerve to tell anyone about his plan."

"That's terrible, Leon," said Nathan. With a big grin he added, "So, why didn't you claim her? You'd be quite a catch for this young lady."

Leon, nervous about his secret nuptials, laughed along with everyone else.

"I 'preciate that, but there's more. Her escort's agreement with that mail order company said if she wasn't claimed by Jacob, he was bound to take her to the local saloon where she would work and live out her life."

"So, why bring her here if there was a plan for her future? Was this really necessary?" Adam's skepticism increased by the moment. "Leon?"

"Did you just expect us to take her in?" Clarissa took Adam's arm.

"Listen, folks." Leon turned his back on the attentive youngsters and lowered his voice. "That broker told me all about his company contract. If the groom doesn't show up, he's obliged to leave her at the saloon where she'll become a prostitute. When he started dragging her toward that saloon, she put up a screaming fit. It was a terrible thing to watch. Some lewd ladies from the saloon kept waving their red scarves to welcome her. That's when I told the broker that I'd find her a home in Springdale."

"So...?" asked Nathan.

"When this girl heard my option, she agreed to come with me as long as she didn't have to live in a teepee. I think it helped that I knew Jacob before he died, and that she would live on a farm. What else could I do? What would you have done?"

The tension in the group relaxed a bit, however Adam and Clarissa shared a long look. Adam stared down at the forlorn unclaimed bride.

"Well, Miss Gisela, welcome to Springdale and Fresh Meadows Farm." He turned aside and spoke quietly to Leon. "For now Jacob's intended has a home at Fresh Meadows. It's the least we can do to honor his memory. But you'll have to work out a plan for her in the long term. She's your responsibility."

"Yes, sir, I understand," said Leon with a grimace.

Clarissa chimed in with a quiet comment. "So, let's all welcome Gisela."

Gisela stared around the circle of Leon's greeters. She set everyone somewhat at ease when she curtsied and whispered, "Dankeschoen, Herr Doctor."

"That means 'thank you,'" said Leon, glad to change the subject.

Curious, Sunny reached over to pat Gisela's tan cap. She giggled when this stranger gave her the cap for her unruly curls. When Gisela held out her hands, the smiling child left Leon's arms and went to this newcomer without hesitation.

Clarissa turned to Magnolia. "Please, clean up that room you stayed in before you married Willy. Make Miss Gisela welcome in the kitchen. After dinner, surely she'd appreciate a bath…she certainly needs one. And tomorrow wash everything in her luggage."

"Yes'um, I'll get her settled after I serve your dinner. We jes' have to help Mr. Leon manage this. At least this lady didn't bite him like that big cat did after Miss Rosalie died."

"Yet," Adam said.

"Now, Adam," said Clarissa. "Leon did the right thing. You have to feel for that poor girl. She doesn't know English, is half way around the world from her home, and faced with being turned into a prostitute? Why on earth would a young girl agree to a plan like this?"

"Heaven only knows," said Adam. "Maybe she wasn't given a choice. And with no ability to communicate, how can she tell us?" He looked over at Magnolia. "I'm going to need a strong cup of tea when we get these horses unloaded. Let's go home."

Adam went on to a less stressful topic. "Son, looks like our new rail system provided good transport for our new horses. They're in much better shape than if we'd trailed them overland. Wait until they see their new meadows!"

"I still missed that trail ride," said Nathan.

CHAPTER 7

*A*fter loading the buckboard with supplies for the new horses, Nathan pulled it closer to the crowd. Leon helped Gisela onto a seat beside Nathan and tucked her bedraggled luggage under her feet. He found a blanket to wrap around her against the chilly ride home in the open air. Nathan kept an eye on Wyatt and Wayne as they jumped into the back of the wagon. Miner Boy, Leon's ride home to Fresh Meadows, was still tied to the back of the buckboard.

When Leon noted Gisela still seemed frightened, he put his hand on Nathan's shoulder. "Gisela, Nathan is the doctor's son. He's my friend. SAFE."

"What?" asked Nathan. "She's afraid of me?"

"She's afraid of everything. SAFE is the only word I've found that keeps her from being terrified. Now, let's see what a German farm girl thinks of the big boy?" He led Miner Boy to the front of the wagon near Gisela. "My horse," he said with his hand over his heart.

Her eyes widened. "Schoen! Phantatisch!"

"Watch this, Miss Gisela."

In one easy motion Leon pulled himself bareback onto Miner Boy. When the big stallion spun around and rose on his hind legs to his full height, the new bride clapped her hands and laughed.

"Das Pferd!" She reached out toward the horse.

"Well, I 'swan!" said Willy as Miner Boy nuzzled Gisela's hand. "Looks like that little girl ain't 'fraid of nothin'."

"In two days, I've never heard her laugh or seen her smile," said Leon. "And, Miner Boy seems glad she's here. He's usually not so friendly."

"Don't I knows that!" whispered Willy. Riding Moonlight's colt, he joined Leon as they herded the travel weary horses toward their new home. Everyone enjoyed the scenic ride along River Road toward Fresh Meadows Farm.

Because the new train tracks ran strategically near the docks where barges were unloaded, River Road was fast becoming an important link between the river, the train depot and Springdale. Adam, who had purchased more land along River Road with funds from his parents' estate settlement, watched his acreage increase in value every day.

Gisela kept silent until they paused at Fresh Meadows Farm to let Willy open the gate. The restored plantation house shone in the sunshine at the end of the tree-lined driveway. Sleek horses grazed in the nearby meadows. She covered her mouth for a moment as she stared at the scene before her.

"Herr Leon?" she reached out for his hand. "Dein Bauernhof?"

He pointed to the name on the iron gate over the entrance: Norcutts' Fresh Meadows Farm. "FARM," he said and pointed toward the property in front of them.

Once she understood, she kept smiling and saying, "Du meine Guete" with her hands over her heart. "Schoen."

"She talks funny, Papa," said Sunny, who rode in front of her father on Miner Boy.

"We must teach her our words. Maybe you can help her learn."

"I'll try, Papa."

"I guess she was expecting a different sort of farm," Adam called out as he shooed the new horses toward the back pasture.

While the men took care of the new horses, the women busied themselves in the kitchen. The aroma from Magnolia's beef stew filled the room. Platters of sliced tomatoes and hot corn on the cob waited to be served. Sliced fresh bread was covered with tea towels to keep it moist and warm. Butter and strawberry jam waited in saucers.

Watching as everyone went about their tasks, Gisela stood along the fringe of the kitchen. Though exhausted, she didn't want to miss anything in her new surroundings. To her, the huge plantation kitchen looked like a wonderland.

When she indicated that she would help, Magnolia asked her to fold napkins and set them around the kitchen table for the workers. Finer napkins were needed in the family dining room, and Clarissa came alongside to help her. Each place around the large table had its own initialed sterling silver napkin ring, a luxury foreign to a German farm girl.

The activities in the dining room and the kitchen overwhelmed Gisela. On her poor farm, their meals were served in a shallow wooden bowl with a chunk of dark bread and a well-worn spoon or fork, never a napkin.

The kindness of the people around her surprised her. In her family, her father and older brothers came in from work, sat down, and complained about whatever she served. After the evening meal, they lolled around the fireplace or went into town to drink dark local beer. They left her by herself to clean up the kitchen. Little more than a child, she would put herself to bed and weep for her mother whose sweet spirit was lost to consumption two years before.

Now at Fresh Meadows, watching the process of a loving American family's meal set her to weeping again. Where did all this food come from? Why did everyone treat her with such kindness? And mostly, why would a farm workman bring her to this place?

Polly noticed Gisela's tears and went to her with a warm hug and a handkerchief. "You'll be all right here. I hope we can be friends. All I have is brothers and Sunny is too young to share secrets."

Gisela tried to thank Polly, whose kind intentions were obvious.

When Magnolia told Clarissa that dinner was ready, the Fresh Meadows family gathered in the dining room. The Norcutts stood behind their chairs while everyone else stood along the back wall. Leon nodded his welcome as Magnolia brought Gisela in with her.

Adam offered a prayer, "Heavenly Father, thank you for our food. Thank you that Leon and our new horses arrived safely. We ask that you bless Miss Gisela during her stay with us. May we serve you well with the strength this food provides. Amen."

The Fresh Meadows workers tried to adjust to this newcomer inside their close knit group. At the kitchen table, Leon sat beside Gisela and told her the names of each item, which she tried to repeat. The others around the table were fascinated by this interchange, and their friendly banter at his expense kept Leon squirming.

CHAPTER 8

After dinner, Clarissa asked Gisela, "Would you like a bath?" When Gisela didn't understand, Clarissa took her to see an enclosure off the kitchen with a large metal tub and an ample supply of soap and towels.

"Ja, Ja," replied Gisela. "Danke." She blushed and looked down at her disheveled appearance. Once again her tears started, but this time they were tears of embarrassment mixed with thanksgiving.

"Very well, we'll bring some hot water for you."

She asked Willy and Marcus to pump enough water to fill the kettle that hung inside the kitchen fireplace. Two smaller kettles rested near the flames.

Over the next hour, Gisela helped clear the dinner tables and scraped the leftovers into a big granite pan for the farm dogs. While she talked to them, the hungry animals waited by her side. They responded to her as a long, lost friend.

"Those mutts must know German," Marcus noted as he and Leon carried buckets of steaming water to Gisela's bath.

"Looks like you're right," said Leon. "You know, it can't be easy to suddenly find yourself in a place where no one speaks your language."

"You two seem to manage all right." Marcus punched Leon in the ribs.

"Cut it out. I just met her this morning before that train left for Springdale. I tried to teach her some words on the trip home. She seems like a smart girl, so she'll probably learn English quickly."

"Why in the world would Jacob order a bride from Germany and never mention it to anyone?"

"Surely he told his son or his brother. They're a pretty close-knit family."

"And something else," said Marcus. "Where'd Jake get enough money for a mail order bride anyway?"

"I hadn't thought about that. A bride like this can't be cheap!"

"Magnolia, we filled that tub for Miss Gisela," said Leon.

"All right. When she's done, I'll fetch her something of Miss Polly's to wear."

"It's up to you to help her from now on," Leon said.

"I knows that. Now you boys go on away."

She led Gisela to the steaming tub and kept humming old hymns to put her at ease. With gestures, she told her that she would shampoo her hair. When the long blond hair was clean, she handed Gisela a bone-handled comb and left her alone to bathe. But not before she added another kettle of warm water.

When Clarissa came into the kitchen to talk about the details for their supper, she noticed Gisela wasn't around.

"Did our visitor finish her bath?"

"Things been awful quiet in yonder, but she had some mighty thick hair to comb out. I ain't never seen so much hair that color."

"Let's see if she's all right. A bath shouldn't take this long."

After some knocks on the door with no response, Clarissa called to her. "Gisela? Are you all right? We're worried about you."

When they opened the door, Gisela grabbed a towel to cover herself. Her lips were almost blue, and she couldn't stop shivering.

"Miz Norcutt, she been sound asleep." Magnolia held up a big towel for Gisela's privacy. "Come wif me, po' thing. Let's sit by that hot fire in yonder so's I can comb out that hair."

Gisela, too sleepy to argue, welcomed the crackling fire and warm blankets. She kept falling asleep as Magnolia combed out her long hair. As soon as the tangles were gone, they hurried across the backyard to the room that would be Gisela's. The room was warm with a fire that Willy had started in the grate of the small fireplace. When she saw a pretty dress of Polly's hanging beside the mirror, she kept whispering her thanks. Magnolia explained with hand motions that she would wash the soiled clothes in her luggage.

"Now you needs to go back to sleep. Over yonder there's a chamber pot under that chair." She helped her into a clean night-gown, pulled back the freshly made bed and tucked her in. "Lawd bless you while you rests up."

The unclaimed mail order bride from Germany slept until just before dawn the next day.

CHAPTER 9

The morning after his return with the new horses, Leon had a long list of chores waiting for him in the barn. First on his list, the new horses needed to be acclimated to their new surroundings. Excited about the challenge, he washed up at the outdoor sink used by the Fresh Meadows employees. Not wanting to waken Sunny, he dressed quietly. He knew his little girl would go straight to Magnolia in the warm kitchen for her breakfast.

He took a quick look in the mirror to be sure his hair was smoothed down. Nathan's prediction proved true at the sale. Several women smiled up at him and chatted while they admired his new horses. He wasn't used to female attention, but had to admit he enjoyed it. He stuffed the German/English dictionary into his back pocket and hurried out.

As he entered the barn, he heard the soft sounds of a woman singing. Through the dusty barn, the early sunlight shown on a dress he recognized.

"Polly, what on earth are you doing out here so early?"

"Herr Leon!" Surprised to see him, Gisela jumped in surprise. "Guten Tag!"

"Holy…! Gisela? Why are you out here wearing Polly's clothes? You scared me half to death. No one is allowed around my stallion or near these new horses. You could've been hurt."

Gisela spread her hands in apology. With gestures, she tried to explain that she came out to brush down Miner Boy for the day. The big horse looked out over her shoulder. His message was clear, "I like this young lady's attention."

"Gisela, Miner Boy's a stallion. He can be rambunctious and dangerous."

She continued brushing the horse while Leon stood close by. Clearly, she knew what she was doing, so he began tending his new stock and the regular residents still in their stalls. He always felt a bit of sadness whenever he passed by one empty stall. Standard no longer occupied his place of honor in the stable. The faithful horse had to be put down last winter after a bad fall on the ice.

Leon returned to Miner Boy's stall with a bucket of feed, but Gisela pointed to herself and then to the food. She had already fed the big horse.

"So, if you please? Shall we let him out into the paddock?" Trying to be pleasant, he opened the door of the stall and pointed outside.

Instead, Gisela indicated that Leon should follow her. She led Miner Boy out into the pasture, not the paddock. With a quick run, she grabbed his mane and scrambled up onto his back. The horse stood motionless until she guided him forward with her knees. Enjoying the early morning sunshine, the pair galloped around the field. Her blonde hair spread out like a cloud behind her.

"How can she possibly ride that horse in skirts and without a saddle or a bridle? And who knew that silly little tan cap of hers held all that hair?"

Leon stood motionless but didn't halt the surprising ride of the mail order bride...of his. She couldn't speak English, but her way with Miner Boy spoke well of her abilities around horses. Leon returned her wave when she waved to him from the far corner of the pasture.

Unbeknownst to anyone outside, Adam, still in his nightshirt, watched from an upstairs window as this scene in his best meadow unfolded. He dressed in a hurry and rushed downstairs. Now he disliked their new arrival even more.

Willy came over beside Leon. "Mr. Leon," he whispered. "You don't want to see what's coming. Oooh-weeee!"

"What's that?" He never looked away from Miner Boy and his rider.

"Mr. Doctor be comin' yo' way. He be steaming mad 'bout something."

"So, what's bothering him?" He waved again to Gisela.

"I reckon you be lookin' at it out yonder."

Leon turned to see Dr. Norcutt rushing toward them with his blue eyes blazing. His anger was no secret.

"Young man, are you daft?" He pointed a stiff finger in Leon's face and waved with his other hand toward the pasture.

"I hope not, Dr. Norcutt."

"Willy, are you a part of this?"

"Sir, I ain't quite sure."

Facing the two men, Adam explained the focus of his anger.

"In no way can I have that girl riding our horses around this pasture! Unsupervised! And certainly not without proper gear or clothing. And absolutely not without my permission. Am I making myself clear?"

"Yes, sir," the men replied in unison.

"Leon, can you explain how this has happened? Why did you allow this Miss Gisela to ride your stallion? Even if he is your stallion, this is not allowed on my property." He emphasized "your" and "my."

"Doc, it's not exactly what it looks like." Leon waved to Gisela to join them at the fence. "I can tell you what happened."

"Well...."

"When I came to the barn, I found Miss Gisela singing, of all things, to Miner Boy and brushing him down. She'd already fed him. She went on and on in that language of hers. When I told her to get away from the stallion so I could take him out to the paddock, she insisted on leading him to the pasture. She opened the gate, gave a run at him and was galloping around the pasture with no help from me. Honest."

"For the love of God, why didn't you stop her?"

"They were out there before I could do anything. Doc, this bothers me a lot, too. I can't understand what she's saying, but one thing is certain, she's at ease with horses and not the least bit afraid of Miner Boy."

"Didn't you say she was a farm girl? The working horses on German farms can be huge...certainly larger than my British polo ponies. Maybe this size horse is what she's used to?"

34

"Maybe so, I don't know. The little I know about her background is what her escort told me all in a rush. He was just glad to get rid of her because she wasn't going to that saloon without a big, loud tussle. I hope I did the right thing, but I'll have to live with it now."

"I suppose so, Leon. But I think that marriage shyster took advantage of your good nature, don't you?"

"Probably, but I had a miserable childhood because men took advantage of my mother. Somehow I had to find a way out of a life as male 'entertainment' for this helpless girl. I guess I was saying that Blue Lark's sad life shouldn't happen again."

"That does shed some light on why you'd rush into something like this."

Now Gisela stood beside the men at the fence and Miner Boy trotted off. With hand motions, she tried to apologize, then began to act out something that made no sense to Adam or Leon.

Willy nudged Leon. "She be sayin' she can milk them cows."

Leon laughed with relief. "Doc, she's saying she'll help with the milking."

"Well, good for her." His clipped voice still reflected his reservations.

Magnolia called to them from the dogtrot. "Gentlemen! Breakfast gittin' stone cold."

"Right now I must join Mrs. Norcutt," said Adam. "We'll talk more later."

"Thanks for understanding, Doc," said Leon. "If you'll approve it, I've thought of a way to provide for this girl...until I find her a place of her own."

As they walked toward their waiting breakfast, Adam clapped Leon on the shoulder. The bewildered girl stood stock still by the fence until Leon waved for her to come along. He paused a moment to look in the little dictionary.

"Fruhstuck!" he called out.

She laughed at his feeble attempt to say the strange word. When she caught up with him, he handed her their dictionary and pointed out the word.

"Now you say 'breakfast.'"

She tried, then ran toward the kitchen as the men laughed.

"Doc, what'll happen when she rests up from all this? Lord help us, what have I done?"

"We'll find that out one day at a time. Let's hope she has a good heart."

"I believe she does."

"Let's discuss your plans for her before I leave for town today."

"Greet Mrs. Norcutt for me, and thank her for helping Gisela get settled yesterday."

The men parted ways, but both had the same issue on their minds: Gisela?

CHAPTER 10

As soon as the breakfast dishes were washed and put away, Sunny grabbed Gisela's hand.

"I'm Sunny. Papa says to teach you our words. Come on."

The little girl giggled and pulled Gisela toward the front yard. Not sure what Sunny wanted, Gisela followed beside her. Along the way Sunny pointed to objects and said their words in English. Gisela tried to say each word back to her small tutor.

After exhausting things outside the house, Sunny knocked on the front door and took Gisela's hand. When Magnolia answered door, she asked, "May Miss Gisela and I come in? I'm teaching her words."

"Baby, what on earth you mean?"

"Papa said I should teach her our words 'cause we can't figure out what she says. I've told her outside words, so now may we come in?"

"Well, bless your heart, come right in. I'll just go along with you so nothin' gets broke."

The trio wandered through the downstairs rooms as Sunny called out words. Enjoying the challenge, Gisela tried her best to imitate the sounds of each word.

"Sunny, why are you in here?" Leon came in for his meeting with Adam.

"I'm teaching her words like you told me to," said Sunny.

"So, what words have you taught her?"

"I don't know if she 'members any."

"Let's try." Leon began pointing to things. Sunny whispered the English version to Gisela, who tried to say it for him.

"You're a good teacher, Sunny. Now go see if Magnolia made a cake this morning. Maybe you ladies can have a bite while it's is still warm."

"Kuchen? Cake? Ja!" said Gisela, who started running toward the kitchen.

Leon looked at Sunny. "Now how did she learn *that* word?"

"Magnolia taught her." She ran after Gisela.

Adam came downstairs and went right to the point with Leon. "Let's hear your ideas for Miss Gisela's stay."

"It's pretty simple. I'll pay her to take care of Sunlight. It won't be much, but if she can live here and have meals, I can afford it."

"Sounds like a decent plan. Have you mentioned this to her?"

"No, but I'll try to explain it to her. Honest, Doc, I have no idea how long she'll be here. If we can give her a safe place until she adjusts and learns the language, let's just see what God provides."

"I still can't understand why you brought her here. You really took a risk and it's not over. For all we know, she could be a thief or have a disease."

"I think about that a lot. I hope I did the right thing. So far, she seems to be a good sort."

"Let me know if this Gisela agrees with your plan."

"Yes, sir, I will."

"By the way, thank you for filling in for me at that big sale. You did an excellent job. Those new horses are beautiful."

"Glad to help out and I appreciate the new clothes." He hung his head. "I didn't know I needed them."

"You're welcome. And to be honest, that German filly you brought us is…interesting." Raising a skeptical eyebrow, Adam turned and walked to the barn where Fancy was saddled and waiting to take him to his day at the clinic.

After her lesson with Sunny, Gisela went to her room and sorted through her belongings. Her tears came again when she discovered a ripped seam in her only nice dress. Her mother had made it with ample room for her to grow into as a young girl. Even with that advantage, the dress no longer fit. Running with her dress to the kitchen, she searched for a solution.

"What you looking for, Miss Gisela?" Magnolia asked when she saw their new resident looking through the shelves over the laundry tubs. "Why you so upset? I didn't want to wash that good dress along with everything else in your luggage. Most yo' clothes be drying on the line."

Frustrated with the language, Gisela answered by rolling her eyes. Finally, by making sewing motions over her torn dress, Magnolia understood.

"Here, look in these baskets for whatever you needs." She pointed to Clarissa's sewing supplies. "Now, sit down with your mending right here." She patted a comfortable chair. "I can use some company."

Gisela mended the tear, eased the seams in the bodice of her dress and finished some other mending her tattered clothing needed. Wanting to make herself useful, she saw a stack of Norcutt mending nearby. While she tried to understand what Magnolia was saying, she kept her hands busy repairing the family's damaged clothing.

Later, Clarissa searched through her sewing supplies for a button she needed to sew onto Adam's shirt for the next day. As she rummaged, she saw the finished mending.

"Magnolia, you did a wonderful job on this mending."

"I didn't touch them things. Miss Gisela asked me for a needle and thread to mend her raggedy dress, but I never saw her start in on that mending of yours. I'll tell her not to touch it next time."

"Good gracious, don't do that. Before I married the doctor, I took in mending only to support Polly and myself. Now with this big family, mending has come back to haunt me. I'm so happy for that girl's help. She's really quite good. Look, her stitches are perfect. She even found scraps in my basket to patch some tears. She keeps surprising us, doesn't she?"

"You right 'bout that, Miss Clarissa."

That evening Clarissa found Gisela to thank her for mending the basketful of clothing. She pulled her into the kitchen and pointed to the mended clothing.

"I know you can't understand me, but I appreciate your mending. Thank you."

Misunderstanding Clarissa's compliments, the girl began profusely apologizing.

"Leon," Clarissa called out. "Please come to the kitchen. I'm trying to thank this girl for doing my mending, but she thinks I'm angry."

Puzzled, Leon stood beside Gisela and tried to calm her down. Finally, he pointed to the mending and said, "Gut."

Clarissa followed with "Good."

Relief poured over Gisela's countenance and she said, "I …," followed by sewing motions and pointing to Clarissa's sewing supplies. "Meine Mutter." She went on and on as she tried to tell them that her mother sewed to make money.

Leon still frantically searching the dictionary said, "I think she means her mother was a seamstress and taught her to sew."

"Well, I never," said Clarissa. "Leon, if she's a seamstress, don't you think we should take her to see my sewing shop?"

"We?"

"Yes, tomorrow you and Fancy can take us in the buggy. Gisela needs to know there is more to Springdale than our plantation. You can drive us around the town, stop by Dr. Norcutt's clinic and visit my boutique on the way home."

"Not sure I can take off, Miss Clarissa. Doc has asked Willy and me to.…"

"Leon, don't worry. I'll tell Dr. Norcutt we're taking Gisela to town tomorrow. Now explain to her that we'll leave right after breakfast."

"Yes, ma'am," he muttered as he turned to Gisela.

After fumbling through the dictionary, he conveyed Clarissa's invitation to Gisela. She started bouncing up and down with excitement but kept asking him something that was obviously important to her.

"Das Kleid? Fraulein Polly?" she asked several times with hand motions.

He finally understood and whispered to Sunny, "I'll bet she's worried about what to wear." He cleared his throat and asked, "You want to wear Polly's dress?"

"Yes, Mr. Leon!" she said in her best English while vigorously shaking his hand in gratitude.

"Of course you can," he said. "She gave it to you."

He turned to leave, but stared a moment at his hand, still warm with Gisela's thanks.

CHAPTER 11

With no way to avoid the trip with the ladies into Springdale, Leon guided Fancy and the rig down the plantation driveway and onto River Road. He hoped Gisela would sit quietly along the way, but this was not to be.

"Meine Guete," she said over and over again. He lost track of how many questions she asked while trying to guide the rig.

"Mrs. Norcutt, I can't get you ladies around town safely and search in the dictionary for the answers to all Miss Gisela's questions." He handed their little dictionary over to Clarissa. "Why don't you give it a try?"

Clarissa did her best to keep up with Gisela's excitement.

"You ask too many questions in your funny talk," said Sunny and put her hand over Gisela's mouth. They both laughed, and the new visitor to Springdale stopped some of her endless questions.

When they came into town, Gisela saw the town hall and whispered, "Rathaus?" Clarissa looked up the word and agreed with her. Another word she confirmed was "Laden" when they passed by The Mercantile General Store.

"Wait here for a minute. Don't get out of the buggy." Leon tied up in front of the store. "Give me one of your shoes, Miss Gisela."

Gisela hesitated, but handed over one of her tattered shoes.

"Maybe Papa will buy us some candy," Sunny whispered to Gisela.

"Or maybe a pickle," teased Clarissa. "But maybe he's buying something for Gisela."

Leon returned with a red and white striped paper bag full of candy. He knew which sweets Clarissa and Sunny preferred, and remembered that Gisela liked chocolate.

"Lecker!" she said. "Dankeschoen, Herr Leon."

When Leon handed her a pair of new shoes, she could barely convey her gratitude. She reached over for the red bandana around his neck to dry her tears and bowed her head in thanks.

"Danke Gott."

"And thank you for all these special treats, Herr Leon," said Clarissa. "Now that you've spoiled our dinner, let's move along to the Springdale Clinic. We still need to stop by my boutique. Or you could bring us back later this afternoon?"

"Springdale Clinic coming right up, Miss Clarissa." He didn't want to spend his afternoon in the buggy with three women. One morning was enough.

At the Springdale Clinic, Gisela paused to put on her new shoes while Clarissa checked them for a fit. Pleased with the nicest shoes she'd ever owned, she ran to the signs in the yard.

"Herr Doktor...Mayor? Buergermeister?" She put her hand over her heart and shook her head in disbelief.

Leon herded his little flock into the clinic. Memories flooded over him as he remembered being there when Dr. Adam told him his mother, Blue Lark, was dying. He still remembered her every day...especially when he noted her Shawnee features in Sunny.

Adam greeted them and encouraged them to walk around his world. Gisela quickly understood where they were. The sights and smells of a clinic are the same in any land. But she was curious and asked a question.

"Herr Doktor, Medizner? Universitaet?"

When Adam understood her question, he explained, "Years ago, I studied to be a doctor in England."

Gisela wandered around some more, then asked, "Mayor?"

Adam pointed to himself and shrugged. Everyone laughed when Gisela put her hand on her forehead in disbelief.

The group hurried on to the Ladies' Fashion Boutique. Clarissa opened the door and greeted her seamstresses. Their finished dresses hung on fashionable stands around the room. Fabrics and laces filled several shelves. Drawings of stylish clothing covered a nearby table.

"Welcome to my little dress shop, Miss Gisela. We make ladies' dresses here."

Gisela stood still a moment, then ran around the room inspecting everything. She especially admired the imported silks and brocades. She grabbed the dictionary from Leon's hand to explain her reaction. The two huddled together until he found the necessary words. He looked up in shock.

"Miss Clarissa, she's trying to tell you that she's a real seamstress. Really—for sure."

"You can do this?" Wide-eyed, Clarissa picked up a detailed lace collar and held it out for Gisela's inspection.

"Ja! Ja! Mit meiner Mutter." She pointed to herself and spun around.

Clarissa chose some yardage of blue chambray and handed it to Gisela. She pointed to the sewing machines the girls operated by foot pedals.

"Here, for a new dress. You may use one of my sewing machines."

Gisela let them know with smiles and curtsies that she understood.

"Leon," said Clarissa. "I think our new friend may have found her niche. If she is as capable as she claims, perhaps she can become a wage earner at my boutique."

Leon's relief was evident as he leaned against the front door frame. Always uncomfortable in the boutique, he was ready to leave. However, he thanked God that they'd uncovered another of Gisela's skills. A place in Springdale for the abandoned daughter of a poor German farmer was becoming more secure every day—just what he had prayed for. As he watched his secret bride's excitement, he thanked God for finding her safe harbor in Springdale. Often consumed with their mutual secret, he pushed it to the back of his mind.

"Lord, what are you doing? And with me? Have Mercy! Just help me know what to do next." With Leon's next thought God provided a possibility which he shared with Clarissa.

"If you want, Miss Clarissa, I could bring her here in the afternoon while Sunny naps."

"Good idea. If she does well making her own dress, I'll know she can manage my demanding customers."

Gisela hugged the fabric for her new dress and kept circling the room. Frustrated, Leon finally grabbed her by the hand and pulled her toward the door. He was ready to leave the female atmosphere.

"I'll bring you back soon. Let's go." The seamstresses giggled and waved to him as he left with his entourage.

That afternoon, Gisela rummaged around in Clarissa's sewing cabinet for the supplies she needed. After setting out thread, scissors and a measuring tape, she drew a sketch of what her dress would look like. That evening she showed her drawing to Clarissa.

"My, my! Miss Gisela, you really do know what you're doing."

CHAPTER 12

On Sunday morning the Fresh Meadows family sat in their accustomed pew near the piano at the Trinity Community Church. Clarissa, still the church pianist, played the hymns she and Rev. Steven decided on earlier in the week. As usual, Warren and Wyatt claimed massive amounts of Adam's attention to keep them quiet. Nathan and Polly did their share of entertaining their brothers.

Leon, wearing his new clothes, sat with Sunny on the row behind the Norcutt family. She kept writing numbers and letters on some paper she found in Leon's pocket. Wearing her new blue dress, Gisela sat next to Sunny.

As the sermon was about to begin, Adam helped Clarissa settle close beside him and whispered, "I like it when you wear your Fresh Meadows perfume."

She nudged him. "Don't get distracted in church, Adam." They tried to conceal their laughter.

Gisela kept looking in her mother's worn German Bible for the verses mentioned in the preacher's sermon. Her frustration was evident to Leon, but he was helpless to solve her dilemma. He could barely find anything for himself in an English Bible, certainly not in German.

The solution silently appeared over Gisela's shoulder. Aunt Mag, who noticed the German Bible and Gisela's struggle, reached for the worn Bible. She found the verses, pointed them out, and returned the Bible. She settled back in her pew and looked straight ahead.

Leon, turning to Aunt Mag, whispered, "You know German?"

She leaned in closer. "Yes, all my cookie recipes are in German. That's why no one can copy them."

Leon looked toward heaven. "God? A solution right here in Springdale all along?"

Clarissa turned around with a frown and whispered, "Shhhhhhh!" Her mouth fell open when she noticed Charlie Tinkerslea, the Tinker Man, sitting beside Aunt Mag. She slipped up her hand in a tiny wave. He nodded a greeting, but his eyes never left Rev. Jackson.

Prudence Phillips shook her head in disapproval. No one heard her mutter, "Shouldn't let that old reprobate inside a church house. Mag should be 'shamed of herself."

After the sermon, all stood as the pastor walked to the rear of the church to greet everyone. But no one in the Fresh Meadows family left Gisela and Aunt Mag, who were chatting away like long lost friends...in German. Everyone leaned in to hear Aunt Mag's translation of what Gisela was saying.

"Glory be!" whispered the older lady. She looked at the Norcutts and shook her head in disbelief. "Do you know what this girl's been through? God in Heaven, her papa sold her. She's so sad. Lordy! I've heard something going around town about a mail order bride for Jacob, but I had no idea she was a German girl!"

Adam nudged Leon, "Tell Aunt Mag what you know about Gisela."

As his story unfolded, Gisela kept patting Leon's shoulder and saying, "Sicher."

"Yes, dear, he wouldn't hurt a flea." Acting shy, Leon turned his back to everyone but Gisela and slipped his finger to his lips. She looked away, but not before she slightly nodded.

"Aunt Mag, look at the new dress Gisela made," said Polly. "Mama gave her this fabric to see if she could sew. It even has a pocket and a little bustle in the back!"

"Well, I never," said Aunt Mag. She turned to Gisela and asked her in German if Polly's story was true. Gisela answered by spinning around and holding her skirts out in a curtsy.

When Clarissa saw Charlie Tinkerslea standing nearby, she walked over to welcome him. They struck up a conversation while everyone's attention was focused on Aunt Mag and Gisela.

"How've you been?" asked Clarissa. "I almost didn't recognize you without all your wares."

"Thank you, ma'am. I haven't worn these clothes since Leon's trial."

"Well, they look very nice. And we still remember you. We'll always be thankful for you. When you testified in court, you helped free Leon from a guilty verdict."

"I saw Claude throw Rosalie Featherson in the river. Only I didn't know that was her at the time. It was Nathan who put the pieces together and told the sheriff. I just told that judge what I saw, that's all." He smiled and looked away.

"Well, what you saw just happened to be what kept Leon from hanging. Anyway, shame on us for not inviting you to visit our church before."

"Miss Mag told me she'd feed me dinner, but first I had to come to church with her." He hung his head and cleared his throat. "This morning when I showed up at her house, she sent me out to her pump to clean up. When I came back inside, she sent me out again to shave. It took some doing, but here I am."

"Well, we're certainly glad to see you. I hope you'll come back."

"S'pose I will. I haven't seen the inside of a church since I left Maine."

Aunt Mag spoke to Leon, "Gisela wants to know if she can spend the afternoon with me. I've cooked up a mess of greens and ham hock for Mr. Tankerslea, so there's plenty."

"Of course she can. You're an answer to our prayers. We'll come by later to pick her up."

Leon and Sunny left the churchyard at a fast pace on Miner Boy while the Norcutts stared after Gisela, now walking arm in arm with Aunt Mag. The hungry Tinker Man loosened his collar and walked alongside the ladies. Prudence turned on her heel and walked the other way.

CHAPTER 13

"Come on, Sunny," said Leon. "Let's go over to Aunt Mag's and see if Gisela is ready to come home." Soon the two tied up the rig in front of the small house where Aunt Mag, Gisela, and Charlie Tinkerslea sat in rockers on the front porch.

"Gisela, it's time to come home," Sunny called out and ran up the path.

Gisela picked up Sunny, then pointed to Leon. "Sit, Herr Leon."

Next she spoke to Aunt Mag in German, "Please, tell him what I've told you."

The circle of friends sat and visited for a long time. Sunny entertained herself playing with an active batch of kittens. By the end of the visit, Leon knew a lot more about his mail order bride and Sunny had a new calico kitten.

"Now, Leon," said Aunt Mag. "Gisela will learn English a lot faster if she can go to the preacher's school. A long time ago when he found out I'm from Germany, he told me he knew some German. He still shows off with a phrase or two. I'll bet he'd be willing to help this young lady learn English, don't you?"

"Good idea, I'll talk to him tomorrow. She'll be fine if given some help. I sure could've used some help when I came here to Springdale speaking only Shawnee."

"You're all of a sudden a very busy young lady." Aunt Mag gave Gisela a hug as they walked toward the buggy.

Before leaving, Leon whispered to Aunt Mag, "Ask her to make herself a split riding skirt like Miss Clarissa's. The doctor wants her to have proper riding clothes."

When Gisela heard Leon's request translated into German, her eyes widened, but she answered in perfect English, "Yes, sir, Mr. Leon."

On the way home, Leon told Sunny, "If you bring that kitten to Fresh Meadows, I wager Master Nathan will call her Bonnie."

"Why can't I name her?"

"You'll have to ask him, but his cat was always Bonnie. She followed him all over."

He looked over at Sunny, but she, the kitten and Gisela now slept soundly.

To leave the ladies' naps undisturbed, Leon decided to take a ride out to the Featherson farms. Perhaps Gisela would like to see the farm that would have been hers if Jacob had claimed her at the Lexington depot?

He pulled the rig to a stop in front of Jacob Featherson's abandoned farm. The barking farm dogs from Luke Featherson's yard came over, but they calmed down when Leon spoke to them. The kitten, terrified by the snarling dogs, woke Sunny with her clawing and mewing.

"Hush, little kitty, I won't let them hurt you," said Sunny.

Gisela also stirred and sat up straighter. "Herr Leon?"

"Gisela, this was Jacob Featherson's farm." He tried to explain that this would have been her home. "You would have been his wife here."

When she began to understand, her eyes filled with wonder. She jumped down from the buggy and explored the yard of the run-down farm. Leon showed her the huge barn with its empty stalls for milk cows and work horses. Last, they looked into the windows of the vacant house.

And she wept. She raised tear filled eyes to ask, "My farmer? Herr Featherson?"

"Yes, this was his farm."

When she understood the truth of what she was seeing, she collapsed against Leon and sobbed until she soaked his shirt with her tears. He handed her his red bandana.

"Gisela, someone is coming over." With a raised eyebrow, he pointed to their bare ring fingers.

"Good to see you, Leon. What brings you out our way?" shouted Luke.

"We're out for a Sunday ride. I was showing our visitor around."

Luke looked from Leon to Gisela, "Who do we have here?"

"Gisela, this is Luke, Jacob Featherson's brother. They worked these farms together until Jacob died."

"Nice to make your acquaintance, Miss Gisela," said Luke.

"She's German and doesn't know much English yet."

"Why don't we go sit over on Jacob's porch?"

Luke ushered them through the neglected garden to the dusty rocking chairs on Jacob's front porch.

"So, you're the one who brung this lady to Doc Norcutt's place? We're isolated out here, so we don't get much town news. We heard something 'bout her, but we thought it was just some crazy nonsense about an abandoned girl."

"It's crazy, but it's true. That's where Jacob comes into this story." Leon leaned forward to tell the details of why he rescued Gisela. All the while, she stared at the men with sad blue eyes.

"So, Jake never told you about ordering this bride from Germany?"

"Never! You know I would've talked him out of such a dad blame idea. He needed some sense knocked into him. So, now she'll go back to Germany?"

In quieter tones, Leon explained to him the contract that would've sent Gisela to the local saloon to be a prostitute.

"I can't believe this." Luke looked over at Gisela. "Sorry, miss. Not meaning to say nothin' bad about you."

Luke went on to tell them what happened after Jacob's funeral. "My wife and I came over here to gather up leftover food and look around. While here, we found birth certificates for the whole family. We'd also hoped to find a will, but there was only a scribbled note saying Jake wanted everything left to Joel and 'my wife.' We wondered why he'd say that because his wife, Merle, died years before that note."

"That's it, Luke! He knew this mail order wife from Germany was coming. He didn't want Claude to ever claim ownership of this farm. He was planning a new life with a new bride and Joel," said Leon.

"So, what should I do if that older boy of Jake's ever shows up around here?"

"Sheriff Olsen and I often talk about that. Just don't let him sniff around here. There's a price on his head."

"Do you think Jacob's mail order bride would like to see where he's buried? It's nice out there since we cleaned it up for his funeral."

"Good idea. Some reality like a grave won't hurt."

They walked out the narrow path to the family cemetery near the creek that divided Luke and Jacob's fields. Leon steeled himself before looking at the grave of his beloved, Rosalie, Luke's daughter, who was murdered by Claude, Jacob's son. All stood in silence for a few moments as Gisela stared at the new tombstone imprinted with Jacob's name and life dates.

"Now go home," she said.

After they said goodbye to Luke and walked back to the rig, she thanked Leon for saving her from the Lexington saloon. "That very bad place. Farm safe."

Still crying into his bandana, she climbed into the front seat of buggy with him and leaned against his shoulder. Surprised, he muttered, "I reckon you trust me now."

"Why is she still crying, Papa?" Sunny reached over from the back seat of the buggy and patted Gisela's shoulder. "Did those big dogs scare her?"

"No, the dogs were just doing their job."

"But why's she still crying?"

"Sunny, she's never seen Uncle Jake's farm where she would've been his wife. She came here from far away to marry him, but he died before she arrived. If your Uncle Jake had lived, he would've been waiting for her that day at the train station. That's where I found her and brought her here."

"I'm glad she takes care of me now."

"Me, too."

"Then why can't we make her happy again?"

"Right now she has a sad heart. Let's pray she'll have a happy heart again."

"All right, Papa. But I want her to quit crying."

Gisela straightened up and pulled Sunny into her lap. Gripping Leon's sodden bandana with a fist of white knuckles, she stared at her empty finger.

Out of the blue, Sunny asked, "Papa, will I ever have a new mama?"

"Our mama, Blue Lark, would like that, wouldn't she?"

"I don't remember Mama Blue Lark."

"That's because you were just a baby girl when she died and you became my daughter. Only the good Lord knows the answer to your question."

He hoped she was done with all her questions with no answers. He guided the rig up the long driveway to Fresh Meadows Farm and helped Gisela and Sunny down from the rig.

"Danke, Mr. Leon," whispered Gisela as she hurried off to her room.

But Sunny wasn't finished with her questions.

"Papa, can't Gisela live with us? That way we'd have a mama and she could be happy again."

"That's not possible, Sunny."

"But, Papa, she could sleep in my room if you don't have room for her."

"It just wouldn't work."

"But she might like to live with us, Papa. I'll ask her."

"You mustn't do that, Sunny." He shook his head as he searched for the right words. "You'll just have to take my word for it."

"Are you sure, Papa?"

"Yes, I am. Now show me your new kitten."

The little cat climbed all over his broad shoulders and back into Sunny's lap. He looked around and wondered why the backyard and dog trot were so quiet. Then he remembered that Dr. and Mrs. Norcutt often went to the shanties for a children's clinic on Sunday afternoons. Everyone else was resting.

While Sunny played with the new kitten, Leon sat on the dog-trot and gave in to his sad memories of losing Rosalie Featherson. As he reminisced about their tragic love story, his old anger surfaced about her murder. How could Claude Featherson, Jacob's oldest, kill Rosalie and her ill-conceived baby to cover his own guilt? The questions still haunted him.

"Lord, I'm so empty. Will I ever find anyone to fill my heart like Rosie did?"

Leaning against the hide of the cougar that attacked and almost killed him, he rubbed the ears of the big beast.

"What do you think? Will Sunny ever have a mother?"

CHAPTER 14

$\mathscr{Cl}$arissa assisted Adam at the shanties while he treated a long line of sick children waiting with little patience in their mothers' arms. As the daylight began to fade, the Norcutts realized they could not help all the children, a persistent dilemma on their Sunday afternoon clinics.

Clarissa began stowing away their supplies when a shrill scream pierced the afternoon shadows. Adam looked up from painting a little boy's sore throat.

"Who's screaming?"

An older shanty lady hurried out of the shadows. "Doctor! You gotta come quick. This little mama don't even know she's waitin' on a baby. And now she cain't have it."

"What on earth?" Adam finished with the little boy's sore throat, wiped his hands and hurried toward the screams.

"She be tryin' and tryin' but her baby won't come. She be almost dead and still cryin' with them pains."

Adam rushed toward the laboring girl. He asked the crowd of concerned women to leave the dark shack.

"I can't see a thing in here. We must move her outside."

The women rushed to do as he asked, then gathered around again. Adam bent on his knees to help the poor girl.

"Why, she's just a youngster! How old is she?" Adam looked up at the hovering women who avoided his glance. No one had an answer for him. "Ladies, I can tell she is very young. Am I right about this?"

There was still no answer from the shanty folk. Instead, they backed away.

"Clarissa!" he shouted. "Come over here! Hurry!"

"Where are her parents?" He looked at the remaining women. "This girl needs her mother."

"She ain't got no mama," said the eldest. "She jes' lives in and out of our shanties. She don't b'long to no one."

"We calls her Girlie," added a girl. "She my friend."

The wall of silence continued, but now Clarissa knelt beside him.

"Adam, they're scared. Just deliver her baby."

"I don't think this little girl will make it. Shall we try to save the baby?"

"Of course," hissed Clarissa.

"Then bring me some string and that scalpel from my bag."

She rushed off and hurried back with the needed items. Girlie's mute audience soon heard the tiny cries of a newborn. Adam huddled over the baby as he tied and cut off the cord.

"Well, ladies," he looked up, "Girlie just delivered a very healthy little boy. Is there something we can wrap him in?"

One of the women hurried over with a tattered towel which Clarissa wrapped around the screaming baby boy.

Adam spoke to the people standing around. "I'm so sorry, folks. Girlie is in God's hands now. Her perfect baby boy is fine, but he needs someone to take care of him. Is there a wet nurse for him?"

No one spoke. A few men now stood behind the women. Clarissa turned to the woman who had provided the towel.

"Would one of you take Girlie's baby boy? He's a wonderful gift to this world."

"Ma'am, he may be gift to your world, but no one 'round here wants no extry chile. We all just scrapin' by. Cain't hardly feed ourselves."

Adam and Clarissa stared at each other. He lowered his voice.

"I'm at a loss. If the baby's father isn't around, someone in the girl's family usually takes the baby. But no one seems concerned about this girl or her baby. What should we do?"

"I have no idea, but we must leave before the daylight is gone."

"First, let me see who's willing to bury this poor girl." He turned and announced, "Someone needs to bury Girlie and take her son."

A man raised a shovel. "I dig her grave, but ain't takin' no baby."

He and another man rolled Girlie into a tattered canvas. The shanty folk disappeared into the dense woods. Clarissa stood holding the wailing baby boy.

"Our work is done here." said Adam.

"But what about this baby, Adam?"

"Let's go, Clarissa. You can't rescue everyone. Someone will take him in."

"These folks aren't going to do that, Adam." Clarissa's fury surfaced. "We might as well bury this baby with Girlie."

Adam was equally angry. "So, what do you suggest, love?"

"Magnolia."

"Magnolia?"

"Yes, she told me that she and Willy want a baby."

"And, just how might she feed this one?"

"If Magnolia and Willy take this baby, God will provide for him."

"I hope you're right." Full of doubts, he finished packing their supplies.

Clarissa climbed onto the wagon while Girlie's son settled into her arms.

Adam looked at the brilliant sunset and prayed, "Lord, have mercy! I'm at the end of my rope. There's no way Willy and Magnolia want a newborn. I pray you'll send the solution my Clarissa is hoping for. Just give us a safe trip home."

As Adam turned the wagon onto River Road, an elderly man shuffled out of the shadows. The tinkling of a bell announced his arrival.

"Here, Doc." He handed Adam the end of a rope tied to a small goat.

"You're giving me a goat?"

"Cain't take no baby, but this little mama goat been my pet. Her baby 'most grown now, so I guess she can go feed Girlie's boy." He waved and muttered. "Named Sally."

"Did that man just walk on water?" Adam muttered as he loaded Sally into the back of the wagon.

All the way home, Sally bleated for the young billy she'd just left by the river. Unbeknownst to her, her new baby boy rode in the wagon in front of her. Adam and Clarissa never spoke on the ride back to Fresh Meadows. Both were lost in the same fog of concern.

What if Magnolia and Willy refuse to be parents?

CHAPTER 15

hen the Norcutts' wagon slowed to a stop in the back-yard, Clarissa whispered to Adam, "Distract everyone while I bathe this baby." She ran toward the kitchen.

Willie and Leon came over to help unload Adam's supplies.

"So, why you got us a nanny goat?" asked Willy.

"Not sure yet, Willy. An older man gave her to us when we left the shanties."

"But nobidey 'round here knows how to milk no nanny, Mr. Doctor."

"God will provide, Willy. Or maybe you could learn how?"

"You sounds jus' like Miss Clarissa."

While Adam talked to Willy, Leon carried Adam's supplies into the barn. In the kitchen, Clarissa poured warm water into a basin. As soon as she finished bathing Girlie's baby, he began crying again. She wrapped him in a warm towel, sang to him and tried to calm him.

Leon hurried into the kitchen. "Miss Clarissa? You need some help in here? Did I hear a baby crying?"

"Shh! We have a baby for Willy and Magnolia! Just pray they'll agree to take him."

Out in the backyard, Adam talked to Willy. "Could you ask Magnolia to come out here for a moment?"

"Mr. Doctor, she be takin' her Sunday nap. I can promise you, she don' want me wakin' her up. No, sir, not on no Sunday afternoon."

"She'll forgive you this time."

"So, maybe you go wake her up?"

"That's not such a good idea."

"Miss Clarissa's the only one who might walk out of there in one piece on a Sunday afternoon."

"She'll be here in a minute. I'm sure she'll be willing to take that risk."

Clarissa hid the baby from Willy as she walked down from the dog trot.

"Clary, could you please go wake up Magnolia? Willy swears she won't allow anyone to interrupt her Sunday nap," asked Adam.

"You could take her a gift. Would that help?" asked Clarissa.

"Maybe, but I ain't got no gift, Miz Norcutt."

Adam took the baby from Clarissa and laid him in Willy's arms.

"Now you do. We brought you and Magnolia this little orphan."

"Lawd Jesus! This real? You folks brung us a baby? Sho' nuff?"

"All yours, just born along the river. The young mother died and no one out there would take her baby. An old man gave us his pet goat so your baby could have milk."

"Maggie Girl, wake up!" Willy took off at a run. "Wake up right now! Look what I got us. Lord, have mercy! Mags!"

Adam and Clarissa waited arm in arm in the backyard for what would happen next. Gisela ran over to see what was going on, but Leon held her back.

After a few moments of berating Willy, Magnolia's cries turned to wails of joy. "What? Willy? You got us a baby?"

"Only if you wants it."

"Course I do, but wait a minute." Her voice changed tone. "How'd you git this baby?"

"Mr. Doctor and the missus brought it from the shanties. The little mama just died birthing, so this baby needs us."

"Well, now ain't we blessed? We got us a baby. So, is it a boy or girl?"

"Don' know! Mr. Doctor didn't say."

"Then let's check." Willy leaned over Magnolia's shoulder as she looked under the towel around the baby. "God bless him, Willy. We got us a boy."

Willy and Magnolia's joy roused other folk from their quiet Sunday afternoon. The happy parents showed their son to Sunny and Gisela. Marcus and Plessie weren't far behind. Sally stood by bleating.

Still relying on their tattered dictionary, Leon tried to explain to Gisela about the new baby for Willy and Magnolia. When he explained that the bleating nanny goat was for the baby, she said, "I milk nanny. Willy not worry."

"Willy, did you hear that?" Leon asked. "Gisela can milk that nanny goat."

Meanwhile, Sally looked around her new home. She quit bleating when she discovered Clarissa's colorful petunias.

"Leon, get that goat out of my flowers." Clarissa was not happy. "Now!"

Smiling, Leon handed Sally's rope to Gisela. "Here, this nanny is all yours. Who knew God sent you all the way from Germany to milk a goat?"

When Gisela laughed, Leon realized she understood his remarks. "Finally," he muttered.

"Can I see your baby?" Sunny pulled on Magnolia's arm. "What's his name?"

"We ain't named him yet. Hold on." She and Willy whispered together a moment. "We be calling him 'Jethro.' Before 'mancipation, an old slave named Jethro took care of me when I was just a little orphan."

"Papa, is it all right to be an orphan?"

"You're blessed if someone like Jethro comes along to raise you."

"Then 'Jethro' is a good name. And I'm naming my new kitty 'Girlie' after his shanty mama who went to heaven today."

Leon whispered to Gisela, "Let's hope and pray that Girlie is a girl."

When he started pointing out the words in their dictionary, she laughed and closed the little volume.

"Book not needed."

A father to the fatherless God sets the lonely in families.
Psalms 68:5-6

Part Two

Let us approach the throne of grace with confidence,
so that we may receive mercy and find grace
to help us in our time of need.
Hebrews 4:16

CHAPTER 16

"Take a look at this, Clary," said Adam. Smiling, he handed her a letter written on fine vellum. After noticing the name embossed on the top of the letter, Clarissa asked, "Who on earth is Adele?"

"She's the widow of my good friend, Dr. Hugo Perry, who died last year. Remember, he's the doctor who invited me to America years ago? I ended up staying in Lexington and working alongside him until after The War. With no desire to return to London, I came here to run the Springdale Clinic. And I was blessed to meet you." He pulled her close.

"But I thought you worked for the Confederate Army during The War?"

"I never chose sides. As a favor, I helped Hugo staff his CA surgical tents on the front lines. It didn't matter to me what side his patients were on. I was thankful I could help wounded soldiers and my friend, Hugo."

"But how can you be thankful? You still have horrible nightmares about those days. And, why on earth would a friend ask a favor like that of a visitor?" Her arm reached around his waist.

"Your Civil War broke out while I was visiting. I had no idea that my favor to Hugo would last so long. Honestly, I learned a lot about wounds and surgery in those front line medical tents. Those experiences and all that pressure taught me things I would've never learned anywhere else."

"So, what's on Widow Perry's mind after all these years?" She waved the note.

"Read it, you'll see."

Clarissa quickly read through the short note.

"Well, what a surprise. Hugo Perry's son, Hugh, is now a doctor? And he wants to consider working here? In your clinic?"

"Honestly, I thought he'd end up in London studying surgery like his father. Perhaps Dr. Hugh is the answer to my prayers. I've needed to hire some help."

"You're right about that. You come home exhausted every evening."

"So, shall I invite him to come for a visit?"

"Of course."

Sitting at the writing desk that evening, Adam wrote two notes: one to Adele, thanking her for her letter, and the other to Hugh.

Dear Dr. Perry,

How nice to hear from your mother about your accomplishments. I know she's pleased you have followed your father into the medical profession. What a terrible blow to lose him in his prime. He was the best of us all. I still miss him.

If you are thinking of working in a small town clinic, you are welcome to visit here. These days it's a busy place, so I'd also welcome your assistance. Of course, I'll reimburse you for working in the clinic.

We look forward to getting acquainted with you. Our children, Nathan and Polly, will enjoy showing you around Springdale. They must be close to your age.

We now have train service from Lexington into Springdale, so let us know when you will arrive.

Kind Regards,
Adam Norcutt MD

As Adam sealed the letter with hot wax, Nathan and Polly came into the living room. He announced Dr. Hugh Perry's upcoming visit.

"We're having a visitor soon."

A long silence lingered.

"Well, Pop, are you going to tell us about this mystery guest?" asked Nathan.

"Dr. Hugh Perry, the son of my late friend, Dr. Hugo Perry, wants to visit our Springdale Clinic." He beamed with pride, but Nathan and Polly groaned at the prospects of their father's visitor. "Why on earth would you two dread this doctor's visit?"

"Forgive me, Papa, but I'm already yawning," said Polly.

"Must Polly and I sit in the parlor and endure this visit? You'll just a go on and on about doctoring."

"No, you'll be in charge of entertaining him," Adam teased his children. "I want you to see that he's not bored even for a moment."

"Come on, Pop," said Nathan.

"Do we have to do this?" asked Polly.

Laughing, Clarissa asked, "Why don't you ask how old Dr. Perry is?"

"Oh," said Nathan. "Seems we forgot to inquire. Does this doctor have one or both feet in the grave?"

"Let me ease your misery. Since you've delayed going to college, Dr. Perry is actually younger than you are, son."

Nathan and Polly looked at one another.

"Well," Polly cleared her throat. "If he's that close to my age, he won't be my doctor. No, siree."

"I met him once when I visited the Perrys at their lovely plantation home," said Adam. "At that time, he was an adorable toddler with a head full of blond curls. His father certainly doted on him."

"So, you're saying he's the spoiled child of a wealthy family who lives in a dream world at his parents' fancy mansion?" asked Nathan.

"Sort of like you and Polly," Adam shot back.

"We're leaving." Nathan grabbed Polly's hand and they headed outside to the veranda.

Adam called out. "Why don't you meet him before you condemn him? He may decide to work here at my clinic. I'd be nice to him…just in case."

"Not a chance, Pop."

"Me neither, Papa."

A few days later Adam received a wire from Dr. Hugh Perry.

ARRIVE FRIDAY NOON STOP HUGH PERRY

CHAPTER 17

Sitting double on Fancy, the Norcutt children watched as Dr. Hugh's train approached the Springdale Depot. Leon waited on Miner Boy. Gisela, who had ridden Moonlight into town for the doctor's use, stood by the hitching post.

As the locomotive chugged to a stop, Nathan said over his shoulder.

"Well…here we go, sis."

"No, Nathan. Not 'we.' I'm not entertaining this doctor. You're in charge of this idea of Papa's."

"Nope. You just smile at him with your pretty face aglow. He'll be plenty entertained."

"I'm not that sort and you know it." Flipping her fan shut, she whacked his knuckles.

"Ow!" He sucked on his throbbing knuckle. "Let's give this doctor a good dose of country life. Then we'll see if he wants to come back."

"He's probably a sissy of a city boy. What if he wants us to hire him a buggy when he sees we're on horseback?"

"Listen, you two," said Leon. "I met this man when I was buying horses in Lexington. I can promise you, riding a horse won't be a problem."

"That's a relief," said Nathan as he tied up Fancy.

"I doubt anything fazes him," said Leon.

Nathan reached up to help Polly down from Fancy. She adjusted her bonnet and smoothed her split skirt. Gisela waited beside Moonlight. The greeting party stood at the ready to welcome their guest.

As travelers exited the passenger cars, none resembled the man Nathan and Polly expected. Families with children hurried away. Several older adults on a sightseeing trip made up the rest of the passenger list. Obliging bellboys from The Excelsior Hotel retrieved their luggage. After the locomotive wheezed down, silence enveloped the depot.

"So, where on earth is this doctor?" asked Nathan.

"Just wait. We can't leave yet," said Polly.

But no other passengers appeared.

"Here comes your guest." Leon pointed toward the locomotive.

After waving to the engineer, a tall blonde man ran toward them. "Halloo! I'm coming! I begged a ride up front with the engineer. Fascinating!"

Out of breath, he reached for Nathan's hand. "You must be Nathan and Polly Norcutt. I'm Dr. Hugh Perry!"

When Nathan recovered his composure, he introduced himself and the rest of the folk from Fresh Meadows. "We've all been looking forward to your visit."

Acknowledging his outright lie, Polly jabbed her brother's ribs with her fan.

"And...this is my sweet little sister, Polly. Our right hand man, Leon, is along to help if needed."

"It's very nice to meet all of you." He looked around. "But I have no idea what's become of my luggage."

"Herr Doctor," Gisela called out. She pointed to his bags waiting beside Moonlight.

"How on earth did that girl get my things?"

"That's Gisela. She lives with us at the plantation. She's from Germany." Leon leaned toward Hugh. "But she probably didn't tip that porter when she claimed your luggage."

"Excuse me a moment while I take care of that." When Hugh returned, he hooked his thumbs under his belt and announced, "So, I'm all yours."

"I hope you don't mind riding horses back to Fresh Meadows?" asked Nathan. "We brought our best filly, Moonlight, for you."

"Not a problem," said Hugh. "But I'd rather ride that big pinto. May I?"

Leon cleared his throat. "Well, he's my stallion and a bit hard to manage. I rode him bareback today, so maybe another time?"

Noting Hugh's height, he lowered Moonlight's stirrups and gave her reins to their guest.

"But where are the horses for the rest of you?" asked Hugh.

"Oh, we make do out here in the country," said Nathan as he gave Polly a lift up behind him.

"We're riding Fancy today," said Polly, smiling. "She's Papa's favorite, but he loaned her to us for the morning. Her real name is 'Fancy Petticoats.'"

Leon, on Miner Boy, helped Gisela up behind him. When she nestled in behind him, he cleared his throat and she pulled her shawl between them.

The party rode along River Road toward Fresh Meadows. Polly assumed the role Nathan had suggested for her as she smiled and answered all of Dr. Hugh's questions.

"Will I meet your father today?" asked Hugh.

"Of course, Dr. Hugh. He and Mama are waiting for us. After we have a delicious dinner, you'll have Papa's undivided attention. He can't wait to show you his clinic. That's all he's talked about for days."

"I'm looking forward to a delightful visit," said Hugh.

Leon and Gisela picked up the pace on Miner Boy and passed everyone. Nathan called out to Hugh, "Shall we keep up with those two?"

"Of course, let's go!"

The rest of the scenic trip along the winding road flew by. Willy held open the gate at Fresh Meadows. In the distance, Adam and Clarissa waved from the veranda.

"See, I told you my father would be waiting for you. Welcome to Fresh Meadows, Dr. Hugh," said Polly.

"The pleasure is all mine, I'm sure," said Hugh.

After tying their mounts to the hitching rail, everyone walked toward the plantation house…except for Leon, who led Miner Boy toward the barn before the big horse could cause any trouble.

With a curious smile, Hugh watched Polly and Gisela run off arm and arm.

CHAPTER 18

*D*r. Hugh was warmly greeted by the Norcutt family. As everyone moved inside for Magnolia's feast in the dining room, Hugh tussled with Wyatt and Warren. Adam's pleasure over their visitor was evident.

"Dr. Hugh, I can't tell you how pleased we are to have you here. I know you want to visit our Springdale Clinic, but first let's have some dinner. I'll introduce you to my medical world later this afternoon."

"I'm happy to be here. My father spoke so highly of you. I remember you visited us once in Lexington. Of course, that was long before I decided to study medicine. Once I chose this path, my father supported me every step of the way until his untimely death."

"We're honored to have you, Dr. Hugh. Now let's thank the dear Lord for your safe arrival and Magnolia's dinner." Adam's prayer went on so long that Clarissa nudged him.

As the well-fed diners left the table, Hugh spoke to Polly. "I've never been around such a large family. Being an only child, I'm a bit overwhelmed."

"Well, you'll just have to adapt," said Polly. "Later, Papa and I are challenging you and Nathan to a game of badminton. Are you up for that?"

"We have a badminton set at home, but we've never used it."

"Just looking at that old set won't teach you how to play the game. But by the end of today, we'll have tested your badminton mettle."

"That's frightening," said Hugh.

"Well, no one is born knowing how to play badminton. So?"

"I guess you have a game, little sister!"

"If you can't manage it, I can always ask Gisela to fill in for you."

"You mean that little German girl?"

"Don't underestimate her, Dr. Hugh."

"Tell her to be ready when you drop out, Miss Polly."

"Not a chance, Dr. Hugh."

While Adam waited for Hugh to change out of his travel clothes, he and Clarissa chatted about their new arrival.

"Hugh seems like an exceptional young man," said Clarissa. "But he's so young. How can he possibly be a qualified physician?"

"I had that same concern, so I wired a friend at Hugo's hospital. He answered back with nothing but praise for the young Dr. Perry. That he's a bit green is a given, but he's definitely qualified for our situation."

"Listen, Adam, you know better than anyone that you can't predict what will turn up at your clinic. What if he takes on more than he can handle?"

"I'll be here to back him up. I'll also tell him there's a qualified local nurse who can step in at any given moment."

"You give me too much credit, Dr. Norcutt." said Clarissa. "By the way, those wonderful blue eyes of Dr. Hugh's rival yours."

Their conversation stopped when they heard Magnolia trying to comfort her screaming son. She paced back and forth on the dog trot as she patted him, sang to him, and prayed, "Now, Lord, what does I do for this po' soul?"

"How is the new mother coping with this baby, Clarissa? He cries a lot, which isn't that unusual. But I'm concerned that her duties as a mother and her role in our household are a bit too much for her right now."

"She's assured me that the pleasure of having Jethro is worth every minute of time he takes. I suggested Gisela tend him for a few hours a day. She agreed, but when I mentioned Gisela could do some of the cooking, she assured me that our visitor is a terrible cook."

"Sorry to hear that. I was looking forward to some German food."

"I'll see if Magnolia will let her try, at least once."

"Tell her I've requested it."

"That just might work. Also, I'll try to be in the kitchen a bit more. Maybe it's time for some of my chicken and dumplings? And perhaps I can rock that adorable baby you rescued."

"Wrong. You came to his rescue and you know it." He leaned in to kiss her.

The doctors rode at a leisurely pace toward town.

"Hugh, since we have a few minutes before we reach town, let me explain why a London surgeon ended up out here in a small Kentucky clinic."

"When you came to this remote area, it must've been quite a challenge."

"You're right. When your father invited me to come visit him in Lexington, I jumped at the chance for a trip to America. He had frequently asked me to cross the Atlantic and work alongside him, but I only considered that a faint possibility."

"So, what was the tipping point?"

"At the time, I was estranged from my wife in England. I missed my little boy and my life in London. I was the proverbial lost soul looking for a new beginning. That I would end up in the CA medical tents and not return to London never occurred to me. When I left London bound for America, I was simply on a bit of a lark." Adam glanced at Hugh. "I hope that doesn't disappoint you?"

"No, sir. It's rather reassuring."

"How so?"

"I'm on a bit of a lark myself. But I still have a question. Why not practice in Lexington or London?"

"Good question. When The War broke out during my visit, your father begged me to serve in his hospital tents on the front lines of the conflict. As his friend, I was glad to help. I ended up spending long months in constant danger near the action. When the conflict was over, I was disillusioned and exhausted. I almost left medicine completely."

"My father also reminisced about the horrors of The War. To my mother's frustration, he drank a bit too much to overcome those awful memories."

"I'm not surprised to hear that. Occasionally I did the same, and frequently with your father, who shared his excellent liquor cabinet with me. I was also often a guest at their wonderful parties."

"My mother loved to entertain in those days."

"At one of her lavish parties, I met Dr. Angus Logan, who ran a small clinic in the middle of nowhere. He wanted to sell his clinic in Springdale, and I found myself drawn to the simpler life here. I preferred the prospects of helping families with routine medical issues over doing surgery every day in Lexington. Hugo's offer was generous, but after The War, I'd done enough surgeries to last a lifetime."

"So, Springdale is where you recovered?"

"Yes, and then I met a pretty little widow named Clarissa. She continues to be my delight after all these years."

When the men tied up in front of the Springdale Clinic, Hugh stared at the signs in the front yard.

"You're also the mayor here, Dr. Norcutt?"

"Yes, but I'll tell you about that later. Right now I want to show you my clinic. It began right here in a small corner of Dr. Logan's home, and grew to be his pride and joy. After buying his practice, I also worked and lived here. Later when Clarissa and I married, we moved with our children to Fresh Meadows Farm. The apartment here isn't fancy, but with some freshening up, it's yours if you stay."

"That's very generous. Thank you, Dr. Adam."

"Come in and have a look around. Feel free to peer into anything. I'm well-supplied for my needs, but I'll supply whatever you might request…within reason. Of course, you may also bring your own equipment. We all have our favorites."

He unlocked the clinic door and held it open for Hugh. Within moments, Dr. Hugh knew he'd found the perfect place to begin his medical career.

"Well, what is your first impression?" Adam asked later as the men rode along River Road back to the plantation.

"Right now, I believe Springdale and your clinic fit me like a glove."

"Good to know." Adam reached across to shake Hugh's hand. "Please, don't feel you have to rush into this decision today. We'll talk more as questions come up during your visit."

The doctors rode in comfortable silence back to Fresh Meadows.

The promised badminton match lasted until the daylight was almost gone. Adam, Nathan, and Polly enjoyed having a fourth to round out their usual family competition. Although Hugh lacked experience in the game, his height and natural athletic ability served him well.

"I'm done. You've worn me out," said Adam after missing a return he normally would've slammed into the corner. "I think I'll turn in. I need to be up and at it tomorrow at the clinic."

"Papa, you can't quit now," said Polly. "It's not fair to stop just because you can't keep up with us."

Hugh leaned over with his hands on his knees. "Miss Polly, I've also had enough. Can we continue this match later in my visit?" Spinning his racquet, he pointed the handle at Nathan. "Until next time."

"Of course, we'll let you retire," said Nathan. "You must also be tired from your travels earlier today."

"Right about that," said Hugh.

Noticing Leon and Gisela still standing nearby, Polly asked, "Would you two like to try the game?"

"Yah!" Gisela challenged Leon, "Herr Leon, I win."

"Not a chance."

"Leon, calm down and don't break any strings!" Adam called from the backdoor. "Please put away the equipment when you're done."

"I don't think this match will last long," said Leon, as he dodged a shuttlecock Gisela aimed at his head.

Inside, Adam spoke to Nathan. "I'll trust you to help Dr. Hugh get settled. I'll see everyone for breakfast in the morning."

"Sir, may I assist you at the clinic tomorrow?" asked Hugh.

"Of course, I'd welcome your help."

As Nathan and Hugh headed upstairs, Polly stood at the bottom of the stairs.

"Good night, Dr. Hugh. Did you enjoy your first day at Fresh Meadows?"

"Yes, Miss Polly, I did." He leaned over the banister and waved.

"Good job, little sis." Nathan smiled down at Polly. "Keep on smiling."

"Just hush," said Polly and stuck out her tongue at her brother.

CHAPTER 19

*T*he Fresh Meadows Farm family slowly absorbed Gisela, their little German intruder. Her skills as a farm worker were evident to all. Her willing spirit and warm heart won over even the most resistant.

Adam admitted to Leon, "Looks like your German visitor has settled down and is doing well. She's definitely trying to do her share around here. Since she started going to school, she's learned English much sooner than I expected."

"Yes, she's excited because she never went to school in Germany. She only learned from her mother. She likes the lessons assigned to your children."

"And what's this I hear? You're staying for school along with Gisela?"

Leon kicked the dirt before he spoke. "At first I went along to help her with the language. But now I stay because I like the lessons."

"Haven't you been to school before?"

"No sir, I just learned whatever I needed to survive."

"But how did you figure things out? You weren't just a workman doing routine chores requiring no English. You had to communicate."

"I figured things out when I had to. I didn't need to know much at first. For some reason, English wasn't that hard for me. As I went along I learned how to make change at the stables, scribble down the names of customers, and use decent manners. Things like that. The stable boss helped me. My mother taught me what she could. She had plenty of Shawnee wisdom, but not the kind of schooling I needed in town. She did teach me about numbers and the few words in English that she knew."

"You're one smart man to have learned all this on your own."

"I just did what I had to do to get by day to day."

"Yes, but not everyone can do that. You're a blessed man."

"Thanks, Doc. It's been a struggle. I've never looked on it as a blessing. Whether I was in Minetown or down the mountain, I've always been happiest working with horses. The rest happened alongside surviving."

"Gisela, could you just stop? I can't keep listening to you and pay attention to what I'm doing here." He was at a tricky point in training the doctor's new black gelding and it was not going well.

"Not like me, Herr Leon?"

"Of course I do. I just wish you didn't chatter all day long. Since you've learned some English, you never stop."

"So, maybe I talk to the chickens or Miner Boy?"

"Why not talk to the ladies at the sewing shop?"

"I do. But I can't tell them our story, can I?"

"No, never tell our secret," he said. "Look, Fraulein, I can't be your best friend. Only girls do that sort of thing."

"Never have best friend."

"Didn't you have girl friends in Germany?"

"I had to stay close to brothers when we go to town. Girls afraid of them."

"Couldn't your parents make your brothers behave?"

"Mother try, but she sick in bed. If I shop for groceries, she send brothers with me to help. But they loud and angry."

"What would they do, Gisela? Did they hurt the girls in town? Hurt you?"

"No, but they were big and dirty. Not nice."

"So, you feared your brothers?"

"No more talk about them."

"Now I know why you were so frightened at the Lexington station. You weren't used to people being kind, were you? Especially men?"

"Only Mutter kind, like angel. She never love Father, but parents need husband for her and he need wife for more children. My brothers not her sons, but she tried. They already very bad boys."

"Did your family go to church?"

"Men work all days. If mother not sick, we go. She told me Bible stories."

"You know, Gisela, we're both blessed to have landed in this good place."

"Yes, but now I not talk to you because you ask me not to talk." She took off running down the pasture. "No way to treat wife, Herr Leon," she called out.

Willy walked out of the barn into the paddock where Leon still worked.

"You need hep' out here, Mr. Leon?"

"No, this black gelding is finally letting me be the boss once in awhile. I don't know why he's been so hard to train."

"Me neither. He's sure a fine one." He hung over the fence and watched for a few minutes. "Can I ask you about somethin'?"

"Sure, what's on your mind?"

"Did Miss Gisela just call herse'f yo' wife?"

Leon took his time bringing the skitterish gelding closer. "Willy, don't worry about what Gisela said. She teases me all the time about marrying her. Since Nathan is going away to school, she says I'm the only man left here. That's all."

"If you say so, boss."

"Maybe Nathan's her best bet for a husband in the long run. Right now, he can't go anywhere because he hasn't sent in his college application. He may just be spittin' in the wind about going to college."

"Mr. Doctor won't be a bit happy 'bout that."

CHAPTER 20

"*S*on," Adam shook Nathan to wake him. "You must post your application today for Virginia Military Academy. They aren't going to hold that scholarship for you forever. They need that paperwork, or they'll give your place to someone else."

"Yes, sir," mumbled Nathan and pulled the pillow over his head.

Adam picked up the pillow and used it with a thump for emphasis. "Bring me the completed paperwork by noon today. I'll be waiting at the clinic."

"Yes, sir. I'll be there."

Nathan always assumed he'd go to the military academy, but for reasons he didn't fully understand, he balked about starting the enrollment process. He dreaded being away from Fresh Meadows. Did they have horses? Were there any girls around? When could he come home? Did he have to bring his own gun? Did he even want to go to a military academy? Could he choose another college? Whenever he thought about all the unknowns of being away from home, he always ended up with a big question.

"Why attend Virginia Military Academy?"

After breakfast Leon asked Nathan for his help with a new horse they'd acquired the day before.

"This one is a handful. Let's try to get him on a lead out in the paddock."

"Sure," said Nathan. "But…"

"But what?"

"Need to meet Pop in town." His gloomy mood was no secret. "By noon."

"What's going on?"

"My college entrance is overdue. Pop wants it posted today. So, I'll help you out for a while, but need to finish that application. I'm not sure where I want to go to school, so this may all be wasted effort."

"Then, don't do it."

"What?"

"What do you want to do with your life? That's the question you need to answer before you go to any school."

"I haven't thought of it that way. Since I was a little boy, I've always assumed I'd go to VMI and into the military. Mama doesn't like the idea because she remembers all the wounded soldiers who suffered during The War."

"What would you really like to do? Be a surgeon like Doc Norcutt?"

"Never. But since that trial when you almost hung for Rosalie's death, I've thought I'd make a good judge. Like that Judge Stallcup. But how do I get there?"

"You need to be honest with your parents and see what they say."

Nathan flipped open the clinic's screen door and stood at the front desk. He kept tapping the brass bell on the counter until his father came out from the examination room with a patient. After the patient hurried out, Adam turned.

"Where on earth have your manners gone? You knew that door was closed for a reason. I was in there with a patient. One ring of the bell is enough no matter what the circumstances."

"Just wanted you to know I was here on time."

"All right, let's see your paperwork." Adam reached out with a grimace.

Nathan handed over his blank Virginia Military Institute registration. "I'm not doing this, Pop. I don't want a career in the military."

"What?" Adam struggled to keep his composure. "Why have you changed your mind? It's a bit late to find another option. Have you told your mother?"

"No sir, I haven't. I didn't know what to say to either of you. All I really like to do is work here with Leon and the horses. I know I need a career—of some sort."

Adam nodded. "Yes, you do. I love this horse farm, but I'd be lost without my clinic. Horses can never distract me from my medical calling. Don't think of getting a degree as a bad thing. Think of it as pursuing something you'll enjoy for the rest of your life. Any ideas?"

"I have an idea, but I don't know how to make it happen."

"So, what's this idea all about?" Adam folded his arms across his white coat and leaned back against the counter. "Tell me your idea."

"It started back at Leon's trial when I presented Claude's gruesome trash before the judge. I was fascinated by how what I said, the evidence I found, and the legal process worked together to free Leon. I'd never seen anything like it. I've always thought I'd like to be a judge...like Judge Stallcup. Remember him?"

"Of course I do. Stallcup faced a horrendous situation that day. He came to a wise, but legal solution. No one could bring back Rosalie Featherson. Thank God, our legal system shut Claude down, and saved Leon from hanging."

"So, how do I get to be a judge like that?"

"You become an attorney. Nathan, you've just defined where you should go to school."

"Where's that?"

"You'll have to study law. It's the foundation of any judge's appointment or election. Harvard is the best place to go."

"But it's so far away."

"With our new rail service, that doesn't present a problem."

"So, what should I do?"

"Go over to the depot and send a wire to Harvard. Tell them you're interested and see what they reply."

That evening when Nathan told his family about his new career plan, no one objected.

"Oh, Nathan," said Clarissa. "I've never wanted you to go into the military. It's so dangerous."

"Clary," Adam interrupted, "Men join the military every day. It's a completely worthy calling. However, Nathan told me earlier today he wants to spend his life as an attorney."

"I had no idea," whispered Clarissa.

"Well, for one, I'm sorry you changed your mind. I thought you'd be mighty handsome in a uniform," teased Polly.

"Just wait until you see me sitting in a courtroom dressed in black robes."

Later that week a return wire for Nathan arrived. Leon, who picked up the telegram from the post office, ran looking for Nathan.

"Nathan? Where are you? You've got a wire."

"Let me see it." Nathan grabbed the envelope and ripped it apart. "Well, well. Leon, I have only you to thank for this."

"For what? What'd I do?"

"Harvard is interested."

"Harvard? Interested in what?"

"Me." He handed telegram to Leon.

NATHAN NORCUTT HAVE ONE VACANCY FOR NEXT YEAR STOP IF INTERESTED APPLY AT ONCE STOP HARVARD REGISTRAR

CHAPTER 21

That same evening, Polly interrupted Clarissa at the piano. "I hate to stop your concert, but I really need to talk to you."

"Mr. Chopin isn't going back to Poland. He'll be right here waiting when I come back. Let's go out on the veranda. The moon should be coming up in a few minutes."

As they settled into the rockers on the porch, they were silent as the moonrise unfolded in front of them.

"So, what's on your mind, sweetheart?" asked Clarissa.

"If Nathan is going to Harvard, what's to become of me when I'm his age?"

"You don't necessarily need an answer to that question right away. You still have some schooling here ahead of you. Many girls go on to fall in love and become homemakers. They are happily settled without more schooling."

"I know, Mama, but there's no one around here I want to marry."

"That's another question you don't have to answer right now."

Polly, quiet a few moments, continued. "Mama, it still bothers me about what happened to you. Look at where we are now...it's like that never happened. But it did, and I'm still that man's child."

"Oh, Polly, you're bound to have questions. So, ask me anything, but don't forget, Pvt. Gary has never been your father."

"I know, but what was he like? What sort of man would attack you? I know I look like him, but am I like him?"

"Let me tell you exactly what happened. I went out back to straighten up an old shed. The man was a drunken soldier who'd found a place to sleep in there. When I opened the door, he attacked me even though I resisted. You've been God's gift to me since that moment. We were blessed that Dr. Adam Norcutt was newly settled at the clinic and was able to deliver you."

"But why would that Yankee soldier do that to you? Or anyone else?"

"I have no idea, Polly."

"He sounds horrible, Mama. But why you?"

"I've asked myself that question a million times, and there's no answer. I learned later that he'd led a troubled life. His problems with alcohol started early and never let up."

"What became of him?"

"He was sent to a military prison to serve out his sentence."

"What sentence?"

"When you were a baby girl, he returned to Springdale and showed up while we were out in the front yard. He tried to pull you out of my arms. Thank God, the Featherson brothers were on the road and heard our screams. They stopped him and took him to Sheriff Olsen. He had a trial here, and then the military put him away. Later, he died in a prison fight."

"He must've been a terrible man," whispered Polly.

"True, but his family always loved him. When they received his belongings from the army, they learned our names from his prison records. That's when your grandmother, Louisa, wrote to me."

"I'm sorry I never met her."

"Me too, but don't forget that God's goodness came out of this bad situation. You have all the best qualities of his wonderful family. Their son had broken their hearts many times throughout his short life. Your Grandmother Louisa often tried to show her concern and love for us."

"I try to remember that all the time."

"When you received the money from Pvt. Gary's estate, I bought the cottage where we were living. My boutique is there now, but it's yours when you have a family and need it."

"I have another question, Mama. Why don't we ever hear from your parents? They're my grandparents, too."

"I'll always be sad that they refused to understand what happened to me and the hard times I went through. I thought having a beautiful granddaughter might soften their frame of mind. I often wrote them, but never heard back. I was notified when my father died years ago, and now I'm told that my mother is bedridden and not expected to live very much longer."

"All in all, I'm so blessed. You and Papa are wonderful parents."

CHAPTER 22

*L*eon tried to contain his foul mood. Once again, Dr. Norcutt wanted him to take Mrs. Norcutt into town. Gisela would also go along. He remembered well the first trip he had made into town with the ladies at Miss Clarissa's request…not actually a request, but one of those things he couldn't turn down.

Now Miss Clarissa wanted Gisela to learn how to help with the shopping. Leon knew she would benefit from this trip, but why did he have to chauffeur these women around? He was manager of Fresh Meadows' horses, not women. Shouldn't the doctor or his son tend to Mrs. Norcutt's requests?

As they worked to hitch Fancy to the buggy for the trip to town, Willy teased him, "It's part of our job, my friend."

Not pleased, Leon added Willy to his list of annoyances. He shouldn't have such a bad attitude, but at the moment he rather enjoyed being annoyed. And to make matters worse, Gisela came bouncing around into the barn.

"Herr Leon, today Miss Clarissa teach me shopping. Then go by myself."

"Well, that will take forever."

"Why you have long face? Be happy I learn." She grabbed his arms for emphasis.

"Just tell Mrs. Norcutt the rig is ready." Not tolerating any more of her joy, he shook off her hands. "Hurry, please."

On their way into town, the women chatted away. With Clarissa pointing out interesting things and translating pertinent words, the trip to town passed quickly. After Leon maneuvered the rig as close as possible to The Mercantile, he assisted the ladies down from the rig.

"Thank you, Herr Leon. You come, too? I need help with baskets."

"I'll return soon to help with that. Don't worry."

Leon held open the door of The Mercantile where the ladies were warmly greeted by Mr. Les, the new haberdasher. After shaking hands with the man who outfitted him with a new wardrobe for the Lexington horse show, he made a quick exit.

Mr. Les spoke directly to Clarissa. "Forgive me, Mrs. Norcutt, but you have no idea who I am, do you?"

"Why, I can't say that I do. Have we met?"

"I was often in your home as a child."

"Now I'm really puzzled, Mr. Les. Tell me more."

"My name is Lester Lewis. Ida Lewis was my mother."

"Oh, my goodness! Lester! You're all grown up. Of course I remember you. Your mother was my best friend. Your parents were so kind to me when I was a poor widow. And now you're running your parents' old store?"

"I remember when you bought that yellow cottage. You were living there with your baby when my father moved us from Springdale. When I saw Polly the other day and heard her name, the light dawned."

"Well, I'm certainly glad to see you. What's brought you back here?"

"After Pop died, we found the deed to this building in his papers. For some reason when he left Springdale, he held onto this building. Lydia and I still can't figure out why he never told us anything about his life here."

Clarissa's old memories of refusing Tom Lewis's loveless marriage proposal too soon after Ida's death came flooding back.

"Didn't he move with you twins to Tuscaloosa to work for his brother?"

"Yes, they ran a big store together. I worked there, too."

"So, what's happened to your father?"

"Pop never married again. He died of a heart attack two years ago."

"I'm so sorry, but it sounds like you and Lydia are doing all right."

"Yes, Pop was a good father. Sis and I had a good home to grow up in. He wanted to send me to college, but I just wanted to work with him at the store."

"After your family left Springdale, several store managers have worked here, but it's never been the same. Now I know why it's starting to look like the place we all loved years ago."

"Thank you, I hope I can do it justice."

"You're doing just fine. Now, please come visit us at out at Fresh Meadows."

"I'd like that. Aunt Mag told me you married that local doctor and have a beautiful home on River Road. Now Lydia is married and expecting her first. After the baby comes, she'll come for a visit and want to see you."

When Gisela cleared her throat, Clarissa remembered why they were there.

"Oh, forgive me, Lester. Meet Miss Gisela who lives with us now. She's from Germany and is still learning English. Today she's here to learn how to shop."

"It'll be my pleasure to show you around, Miss Gisela. Don't hesitate to ask me anything. I'll assist you with the names of items and their prices."

"Danke, Herr Lester. I learn."

"Show me your list and I'll take you around." Gisela followed Mr. Les through the store.

Clarissa had many memories of her friendship with the Lewis family. Her thoughts ran the gamut of happy and sad—from their care for her at her most desperate, to the sudden death of Ida Lewis here at the store, to Tom Lewis's unexpected proposal of marriage. Musty town secrets and tales still hovered in the rafters above the old store. That she could've been Lester's stepmother was one of those secrets.

Leon returned to the store to assist the shoppers. As he watched Mr. Les assisting Gisela, he felt something unexpected grow in his chest. Whatever it was made him want to step between the haber-dasher and his eager little customer.

"Why does she keep smiling up at him? Shouldn't she reject his pushy help? I think he's taken a shine to Gisela. What sort is he? He may be smooth on the outside, but not so nice on the inside? What if Gisela decides she likes him?"

On the ride home, Leon puzzled over his strange feelings. "Why do I care if that Mr. Les is helping Gisela a bit too much? After all, she is my wife in name only. If she finds someone to marry, wouldn't that fit my plan?"

But these strange feelings did not go away. They kept him awake that night. The next morning, Sunny sat on one of the barn railings as Leon and Willy fed and watered the horses.

"Papa, why do you have a frowny face? Why aren't you happy today?"

"I'm fine, Sunny. Just have lots to do today out here in the barn. Run along now. Go ask Magnolia for some hot chocolate. And don't forget to say 'Please.'"

Later Willy leaned toward Leon as they pumped water for the horses.

"I'se just speculatin' like Miss Sunny. Does that frowny face of yours have anything to do with your trip to town with the Missus and Miss Gisela yesterday?"

"Nothing to worry about, Wills. But that Mr. Les at The Mercantile was a bit too sweet on Miss Gisela. He stuck to her like glue. Nothing improper, but I can't get it off my mind."

"Well, ain't you been asking God to find her a husband?"

"Yes, but not this one."

Later Willy told Magnolia, "Gotta watch what's goin' on with Leon and that Miss Gisela. I think his heart's 'bout to get broke."

"He just taking care of her. He's tryin' to find a husband for her, that's all."

"I don't know. Course, I cain't really say nothin' to him."

"Go ahead on. Mr. Leon may need someone to talk to."

"Maybe he talk to you better?"

Magnolia flipped the end of her tea towel at him as he left her kitchen.

CHAPTER 23

After Dr. Hugh discovered Dr. Adam's beautiful horses, he enjoyed spending time at the stables. One day he asked Leon a question.

"Do you remember telling me I might ride Miner Boy someday?"

"Yes, I do."

"I'd still like to give it a try."

Leon hesitated a moment before saying, "Why not? You handle horses well. But I ride him bareback. Can you do that?"

"To be honest, I've never ridden bareback."

"Over his complaints, I've ridden him with a saddle. You're welcome to try it if we can get a saddle on him."

After Miner Boy put up a tussle, Leon tightened the girth on his saddle and said, "Behave, Big Boy." He handed the reins to Dr. Hugh. "First, ride around the paddock so I'll know you can manage him. Then take him up and down River Road or around the pasture."

"I'll stay close by." He sat comfortably on Miner Boy, who fretted a few times at the unusual girth, but settled down.

As he watched Hugh riding off on his horse, Leon recalled the first time he saw the pinto stallion. His dying mother, Blue Lark, had just been taken away by their relatives to die with her Shawnee kin. The relatives had also made an impromptu decision that her baby girl, Sunlight, would now be Leon's child. And then they left.

When Blue Lark's funeral procession was well up the mountain trail, the local laundry lady brought Miner Boy to Leon. Blue Lark wanted her son, not her Shawnee kinfolk, to have her stallion.

On an impulse, Leon jumped bareback onto his gift, and they went on a wild ride throughout the little village. The strength and energy of the horse amazed him. Together, a new father with a toddler and a rambunctious pinto stallion left his childhood home. They travelled through the moonlit night back to Fresh Meadows Farm.

Almost like part of his reverie, Miner Boy abruptly appeared out of nowhere and skidded to a halt in front of Leon. The horse was wild-eyed and without a saddle…or Dr. Hugh.

"What's happened? What have you done?" shouted Leon. "Where's the doctor? Show me where you left him."

He jumped onto Miner Boy. Racing down River Road, Leon saw Gisela and Sunny running toward him. Both were screaming and waving.

"Where's Dr. Hugh? Have you seen him?"

"By creek. Hurt," said Gisela.

"Papa, go help him," cried Sunny.

Gisela tried to explain. "Something broke. Not breathe much. Big hurt."

"Gisela, send help. Tell Willy to bring Dr. Norcutt out from town. Must bring the wagon to the creek. Do you understand what I'm saying?"

Gisela nodded and struggled to catch her breath until Leon shouted, "Go! Now!"

As Leon searched along the creek bed, he found the lost saddle half submerged in the creek, but no sign of Dr. Hugh. The silence of the scene was broken only by the rushing of the creek until he heard a moan. The doctor lay sprawled among tall cattails in some shallow water.

"Dr. Hugh! I'm right here. Let me help you up."

"No! Stop! Pain! Ribs broken." Hugh wrapped his arms around his ribcage to ease the pain. Leon propped him against the saddle.

"Just rest. We must wait until Willy and Dr. Norcutt get here with the wagon."

To Leon's surprise, Clarissa was the first to arrive. As soon as she heard what had happened, she grabbed blankets and the extra black bag Adam kept at home. Rushing to the creek, she found the men.

"Dr. Hugh, you poor man. What happened?"

"Horse reared. Fell on top of me."

"Leon? Have mercy! Should Dr. Hugh be riding this ornery horse of yours? You should know better."

"I'm so sorry, Miss Clarissa. Dr. Hugh's been asking to ride Miner Boy. I finally agreed because he's a good horseman. I watched them in the paddock before I let them leave. Miner Boy has never liked a saddle, but he was behaving when they left."

"Not horse," Hugh whispered. "Big splash scared horse."

"Oh, that's the beavers," said Leon. "They're trying to dam up this creek. Whenever they sense danger, they slap the water with their big tails. Marcus and I need to get rid of them. At the very least, we'll tear down their dam."

"Miss Clarissa?" Hugh could only whisper.

"I'm right here. You just lie still until more help arrives."

"Laudanum in bag?"

"Yes, a small bottle, but Adam doesn't let me give it out."

He pointed to himself, "Know proper dose."

"Of course you do, Dr. Hugh."

The young doctor told her the correct amount and said, "Give half." With some pain relief, he admitted, "Shouldn't doctor self."

"For shame," said Clarissa. "I must report you." Hugh tried not to laugh.

When the men arrived with the wagon, Adam assessed the scene. "First we must move you out of this cold water, Dr. Hugh."

The team of four, Adam, Clarissa, Leon and Willy, rolled Dr. Hugh onto a blanket and pulled him onto the sand bar. After drying him off and bundling him in as many dry layers as they could find, they let him rest and warm up. He couldn't stop shivering.

"When you're ready, we're going to help you onto the back of that wagon."

"I'm ready. Postponing it won't make it any easier," said Hugh.

"Do you need more laudanum?" asked Adam. Hugh refused, and the rescuers pulled him over to the wagon.

"Now you must stand if you can. Willy is right behind you for support. We're here to help you onto the wagon where you can lie down again."

With a large boulder to step up on, Hugh settled into the wagon. His white pallor told his rescuers he was in tremendous pain.

"I don't want you going into shock," said Adam as he tucked more wraps around Hugh's midsection.

"Right," muttered Hugh and reached up to shake Adam's hand.

Adam and Clarissa made a quick assessment of Hugh's situation, and decided it would be best for him to recover from his injuries in his apartment next to the clinic. Adam could keep an eye on him and the hotel could bring him food. Someone from the farm could come by daily to be sure he had all he needed.

After explaining these arrangements to Hugh, Adam said, "Bruised and broken ribs are no fun, but you're going to be all right. When we get you to the clinic and I bind you up, you'll feel a lot better. I don't think your broken ribs have injured you internally."

Willy guided the wagon carefully along River Road, still it was an excruciating trip for Dr. Hugh. When settled into his bed at the clinic, he accepted another dose of laudanum. Adam spent the night there to be sure his young partner was resting comfortably.

CHAPTER 24

When Magnolia heard of the meal plans for Dr. Hugh's recovery, she wouldn't hear of the hotel providing food for the injured doctor. From then on, Hugh dined on the same menu as Fresh Meadows Farm. Whoever delivered his food that day also washed his dishes and picked up his dirty laundry.

After several days into this routine, Polly spoke to Adam. "Papa, my time is free all day. Why don't I make the trip to town with whatever Dr. Hugh needs? That way, no one will have to take time out of their busy schedule, and I can go to town. Moonlight and I will enjoy the trip."

"What a great idea, little sis," said Nathan. "Just keep smiling at Dr. Hugh with that pretty little face of yours all aglow. He'll heal up in no time."

"Hush your mouth, Nathan," Polly hissed. "It's not like that!" She spun around and left.

"Really?" Nathan hollered after her.

That evening, Clarissa questioned the wisdom of Polly's new plan.

"Adam, is it proper for Polly to be alone with Dr. Hugh in his apartment every day?"

"Don't worry, Clary. I've already thought about this and share your concerns. I'll be sure that door between the clinic and Hugh's apartment is open during Polly's visits. Anyway, Hugh Perry is a true gentleman who can barely move with those painful broken ribs."

"I still don't like the idea. There are several people here on the farm who could easily make that trip every day."

"Relax, my dear. You've raised Polly to be a perfect lady no matter what the circumstances. Helping Hugh won't be a problem."

Gisela searched in the barn for Leon. "Herr Leon, where are you?"

"Up here," he called down from overhead. "What's on your mind?"

"Why you so high?" she asked.

"I'm storing hay bales. You need something?"

"Yes. Magnolia send me to town today when Miss Polly takes food to Dr. Hugh. I shop while she helps doctor. You help me at store."

"Haven't I taught you anything, Fraulein?"

"What I do wrong?"

He started laughing. "Say 'please' when you ask me to do something."

Through the dust motes in the attic, she could see him smiling down at her.

"You laugh at me." She turned and ran out of the barn.

"I'll come along," he called after her. "I'll get the rig ready."

All the way into town, Polly and Gisela laughed and shared stories, maybe secrets.

"What are you ladies giggling about? What's so funny?"

"I'm just teasing her," said Polly. "Whenever she comes to town with me to take care of Dr. Hugh, he helps her learn English words. I think she likes him."

"He teaches me new words, Herr Leon," said Gisela. "He nice."

The now familiar wrench in Leon's heart returned. His internal struggle continued, "So, now even Dr. Hugh is helping her? Isn't my teaching enough for her?"

After unloading Polly, along with Dr. Hugh's food and clean clothes, Leon took Gisela into town. "Today I'll come into The Mercantile with you. I'm tired of waiting outside while you and Mr. Les gather up your purchases."

"Don't you go to stables?"

"Not this time."

He went into store with her and rushed to make their choices before Mr. Les could come over to help. Along the way, he tried to teach her the names of the unfamiliar items in the store. When they were done with Magnolia's shopping list, Leon settled the bill with Mr. Les.

"Thank you, Mr. Les. I guess we'll be on our way. We're in a bit of a rush." He reached over for Gisela's elbow and rushed her out the door.

"But...?" said Mr. Les as he waved goodbye at the screened door of The Mercantile.

"Herr Leon, I not in hurry. Wanted to look at chocolates."

"Here." He handed her a small striped sack full of chocolates. "Is this what you wanted?"

Surprised, she looked at him without saying thanks. They sat in silence on the way over to the Springdale Clinic to pick up Polly.

CHAPTER 25

*D*r. Hugh always enjoyed watching Polly as she straight-ened up his apartment, gathered his dirty laundry, and washed his used dishes. Her visits never failed to raise his spirits and he began to look forward to them. One day as he tried to think of a reason to delay her departure, he noticed a book he'd been meaning to read.

"Miss Polly, why don't you stay a bit and read to me. I brought this book from Lexington, but find it hard to concentrate on any-thing these days."

"What a nice idea. Just let me dry my hands."

Reading to Hugh became a regular part of Polly's daily visits. One day, she suggested another activity.

"Papa says you should start walking, so shall we walk a bit?"

"Good idea. I've become lazy. I'm up for a change."

On their daily walks, they talked about many mutual interests. Hugh was surprised she knew so much about horses. He often found her questions about his medical world insightful. On the other hand, Polly felt blessed to be in his company. She enjoyed hearing about his more sophisticated life in Lexington.

"Polly, growing up in Lexington is why I wanted to be a doctor in a small town. I don't want to spend my days like my father did in a hospital and separated from ordinary folk."

"But didn't your father care for his patients?"

"Of course he did. We both did, but I just felt out of place in a hospital. When he told me about his friend's small, rural clinic in Springdale, I couldn't wait to come see it."

"Well, we're certainly glad you came."

"I'm glad to be here, too. And, I want to thank you for taking care of me. Your visits are the highlight of my day."

"You're too kind, Dr. Hugh."

"Not at all. In fact, I'll be up and about soon, and I'd like to call on you sometime. What would you think of that?"

Polly paused as she absorbed the meaning of this question. "I don't know what to say, Dr. Hugh. I had no idea you would want to..." Her words tumbled over each other. "...come calling on me, I mean."

"Wait, Polly," he reached for her hand. "I enjoy your company and you're a lovely young lady. Please say 'yes.'"

Sure her face was crimson, Polly replied. "You'd be most welcome at Fresh Meadows, morning or evening."

"Polly, I'm calling on you, not your house. I've come to care for you. I realize I'm a bit older, but that's not a problem for me. May I ask your father's permission to call on you?"

Speechless for a moment, Polly whispered, "Of course."

They walked into the clinic and waited for Adam to finish with a patient.

"It's good to see you up and about, Hugh. So what's on your mind? Polly?"

"Papa, Hugh wants to ask you something."

Adam looked at Hugh and nodded for him to continue.

"Dr. Adam, I'd like your permission to come calling on Miss Polly."

"Well," Adam cleared his throat. "I see no reason to object. You're welcome to visit Polly any time." After Hugh left, Adam sat a long time staring into space. "Forever more! What on earth will Clarissa think of this?"

After calling on Polly in the evenings for several weeks, Hugh surprised her with a question. "Polly, would you like to spend the day next Saturday with me?"

"But what will we do?" Polly teased. "Sit on the veranda all day?"

"If I had to, I'd enjoy it. But may I plan a day out and about for us?"

"I suppose so."

Polly saw Hugh to the door and wondered what they would do all day together. He also had no idea what they would do. Not well acquainted with the area, he was at a loss. Until....

"Wait a minute! I came here on the train. Maybe a train ride would work?"

When he checked the train schedule at the depot, he found a round trip that would fit his plan. Just to be sure, he checked out his idea with Adam one morning.

"Dr. Adam, may I have your permission to spend this Saturday with Polly?"

"All day?"

"Yes, Polly said she'll trust me to plan the day. But I want my secret plans to meet with your approval." He told Adam about his idea of a train ride.

"Sounds like fun. She'll enjoy that."

When Hugh called on Polly that evening, he told her only a part of his idea.

"Plan to be gone all day to nowhere."

"We're going somewhere together?"

"Yes, bring a wrap in case the weather turns cool. We won't be on horses, so no need to wear that split skirt of yours."

CHAPTER 26

*O*n Saturday morning, Willy and Polly waited with the buggy in front of the Springdale Clinic. She leaned out of the window to watch for Hugh.

"Do you think he's ready?" Polly asked Willy.

"Let's give him a minute. He got this all planned out."

"Well, I can't for the life of me figure out what Dr. Hugh has up his sleeve."

"You ain't gonna be sad 'bout this, Miss Polly. No, siree."

"Oh, my!" Polly quickly sat back into the seat. "He's coming!"

Hugh hurried out to the buggy. "Good morning, Miss Polly. I hope you haven't been waiting long?"

"No, we just arrived. Willy assured me you wouldn't be late."

"So, let's be on our way."

When Willy stopped the rig at the train depot, Hugh handed Polly a ticket.

"This is for me?" Polly asked.

"None other. I'm taking you on a train ride for the day. Along the way, we'll have lunch in the diner car. How do you like my surprise?"

"I don't know what to say. I've never ridden on a train before."

He confirmed the time of their return with Willy, then helped Polly down from the buggy. Too overwhelmed to speak, she took the hand he offered.

"Let's go in and wait for the train to arrive. That's part of the fun."

"But where are we going?"

"This train goes north from here to a crossing with another track. There's a small town there and a yard for holding cattle. The train stops for about an hour to refuel and to let the engineer rest. This afternoon, we'll return along the river back to the depot. Willy will be here waiting for us."

The day went better than Hugh planned. Polly was fascinated by the whole experience. She especially liked dining with him as the miles rolled along. The waiter, in his spotless white jacket, served their meal and refilled their coffee cups from his tall silver coffee pot. Sensing Hugh's desire to impress this pretty young lady, he did his best to make their meal perfect. The other diners tried not to stare, but the romantic atmosphere around Hugh and Polly was no secret.

"Hugh, this is so much fun! How did you ever come up with this idea?"

"This was the best I could do. I honestly wondered if you could tolerate me for an entire day. So far I think we've done all right, don't you?"

"Of course we have. Today just feels like our visits while your sore ribs healed up. Sometimes I felt like I wore out my welcome."

"Those times with you were wonderful. I could completely forget my aches and bruises. Honestly, I never wanted you to leave."

She hesitated to respond. "Well, I'm just glad I could help you feel better."

"Polly, I really like it when you're with me. Don't you ever get tired of me, or want to argue with me?"

Quiet a moment before she answered, she said, "Nathan and I argue all the time, but you and I never do that. We've definitely had some heated debates, but they're more fun than serious. And I certainly don't get tired of you."

"Well, that's a relief."

After the waiter served their dessert and more coffee, he brought the bill on a small silver tray. Hugh thanked him, paid their tab, and left a generous tip.

"Let's stop between the cars on our way back," Hugh suggested. "We'll feel the wind and watch the ground rush beneath us. I'll make sure you won't fall through."

"Glad to hear that, Dr. Hugh." She was fascinated with every detail of her first experience on a train.

"Are you always this excited about a new adventure?"

"This is my first one. I haven't had many adventures. Thank you so much."

They spent a long time standing on the narrow passageway between the cars. Hugh enjoyed this opportunity to hold her against him to keep her steady. Over the clacking of the train tracks beneath them, Hugh shouted to make himself heard.

"Polly, today has convinced me of something I've known for a while. It's something I haven't told you, but I should."

She leaned in to listen to him over the noise of the train, "What's that?"

"I've fallen in love with you. It's high time you know that. I'm not just a flirtatious young boy hoping you'll look my way. I'm a grown man wanting to win your heart."

Polly was speechless for a few moments before she replied. "Hugh, I don't know. I've never had a sweetheart before."

"Haven't all the eligible bachelors in Springdale flocked around you?

"None that I'd be the least bit interested in. And, don't you have girlfriends waiting back in Lexington? Quite a few, I'm sure." She tried not to cry, but reached up her sleeve for her linen hanky just in case. "I'm just not sure about this, Hugh."

Sensing her hesitance, he turned her to him with both arms around her. "Polly, don't worry. At my mother's insistence, I've escorted a few of her choices for me, but none caught my eye. Not like you. Please don't cry."

"I'll try not to. I just am so bad at this."

"You're doing fine, Polly. The more I hold you, the more I want to kiss you. May I?" When she nodded, they quit watching the ground rush beneath them.

The Pullman attendant came out to tell them they were approaching the Springdale depot.

"Let's return to our seats. But I'm not ready for this to end, Miss Polly."

"Dr. Hugh, you came here to work at Papa's clinic. So, this is all a bit of a surprise."

He leaned closer to her blonde curls to whisper, "I enjoy every minute of my work at the clinic with your father, but I've had my eye on you since the day I arrived."

CHAPTER 27

*C*larissa chatted with Adam as they sat out on the dog trot one cool evening while Hugh and Polly visited on the veranda.

"What on earth is going on between those two?" she asked. "This is looking more like a romance than a friendship."

"I've wondered that as well, so I asked him about it the other day. He told me how much he enjoyed her company, but didn't say much more."

"Well, there's a lot more going on! Can't you tell?"

"Now you're acting like a mama hen, Clary. Let's not worry. I think they became friends when she helped him recover from those broken ribs. Polly's a bit too young for someone Hugh's age."

"So? That's honestly what you think?"

"Yes, it is."

"Adam, a mother knows when her daughter is falling in love. Polly has all the earmarks of being smitten and so does he." When Adam didn't say more, she added another detail. "Have you forgotten we're 10 years apart in age? That difference doesn't keep the sparks from flying between us, does it?"

"You'd better not remind me of that. I may take you out to our spot in the moonlight under those pine trees."

"That spot where we both suffered for days afterwards with what Blue Lark called 'Devil Weed'? Without Leon's Shawnee remedy, we'd still be covered with blisters from our evening in the moonlight."

"I've since learned that devil of a weed is better known as 'Poison Ivy.'"

Everyone around Fresh Meadows noticed that a serious romance was in the air. Even though Hugh came to call on Polly, he and Nathan frequently played badminton in the evenings.

"Hugh?" asked Polly, "If you are calling on me, why do you play badminton with my brother all the time? Have your feelings toward me changed?"

"Of course my feelings haven't changed. And Nathan is no competition at all for my affections. Why don't you play with me sometime?"

"Your badminton skills have certainly improved since you arrived in Springdale. You're way too good at the game now. I wouldn't stand a chance against you."

"But I would enjoy playing with you a lot more than with Nathan."

"Tomorrow evening you're on. No more just watching you and my brother play."

Before the sun went down, the entire Fresh Meadows family gathered around to watch the badminton match between Polly and her sweetheart. Nathan appointed himself to be the impartial referee. Leon went from one to another with a pouch and a list in his hand.

"What is Leon doing, Polly? Why are all these people standing around?" Hugh looked around at the crowd.

"When Leon heard about our plans for the evening, he started taking wagers on our match. He even persuaded my parents to participate. The excitement has been building around here all afternoon."

"So, folks are actually betting on our match?"

"Well, Papa put a limit on how much Leon could collect. I'm so sorry, but I had nothing to do with this."

"Well, game on, Miss Polly."

Nathan called on the players. "Let the game begin."

He tossed a coin, and Polly won the toss. From then on, the match moved right along. Polly won a couple of the games, but Hugh ended up with the winning score. After the sweethearts shook hands at the net, Leon moved forward to pay off all the bets.

"Wait, Leon," said Hugh. "There's something I've wanted to do, but I've been waiting for just the right moment. I think this is it."

Leon yielded his place to Hugh.

"Polly, I never thought I'd have an audience for this." He dried his hands on a nearby towel and knelt down in front of her. "Polly Norcutt, will you marry me?"

There was dead silence until someone in the crowd said, "Well?"

Trying to recover from shock, Polly took Hugh's face in her hands. "Yes! Of course!"

Hugh stood and embraced her while the crowd cheered. Adam and Clarissa stepped closer to congratulate them.

"I just have one question for you, Dr. Adam. I haven't asked your permission to marry Polly. So, do I have it?"

"Yes, you do, Dr. Hugh. I never knew I was hiring a husband for Polly when I asked you to work in my clinic."

"I'm equally surprised. This is certainly a benefit of my employment. I do have one question for you. Who was your money on tonight?"

"On Polly, of course. But tonight, you're both winners."

Hugh wrote to tell his mother his good news. His long letter was full of the wonderful reasons why Polly was his choice.

"Mother, now you'll have a daughter to dote on. I can't wait for you to meet her. We haven't set a date, but soon. You'll love my sweet Polly. She already loves you. Don't forget to bring Grandma Perry's ring. I'm ready to see it on Polly's hand. Hurry!"

Adele Perry responded by wire right away:

COMING FOR SHORT VISIT STOP WILL SEND
DETAILS SOON STOP MOTHER

When Adam came into the clinic, Hugh showed him Adele's telegram.

"Wonderful news, Hugh. She can meet Polly, and you can show her the clinic."

"Of course, I've told Mother about Polly, but she wants to meet her."

"Can't blame her for that, can you?"

"Not at all. And I want to show her around Springdale."

"Sometimes folks are surprised we don't live in caves and cook on open fires. When Leon brought Gisela here, she asked if she'd be living in a teepee."

"I'll clean up my spare room so she can stay here with me. We can manage our meals here or eat at the Excelsior."

"I doubt Clarissa will agree. She'll want to host your mother at our home."

However, Adele's own plans arrived in the mail. "I've made reservations at the Excelsior Hotel for my visit."

That night Clarissa mentioned some concerns to Adam. "Why would Adele rather stay at that hotel than with us? Don't you think that's rather strange?"

"I've known her for years. She's always had a mind of her own. Don't worry, there'll be plenty of opportunities to entertain her out here."

On the day Adele was leaving Lexington bound for her Springdale visit, she admired the elaborate diamond ring promised to Hugh in his Grandmother Perry's will. She polished it on her sleeve and slipped it onto her finger to watch it sparkle. Before leaving, she placed the heirloom back into its velvet pouch, returned it to their family safe box, locked it, tucked the key inside her corset and caught the train for Springdale.

CHAPTER 28

*T*he Norcutt family waited with Dr. Hugh at the Springdale depot for the arrival of his mother from Lexington. When the whistle sounded in the distance, everyone moved closer to the tracks.

Hugh rushed onto the train to assist Adele with her luggage and down the steps. She was dressed in a fashionable gray travelling outfit. A large black and blue plume of a feather curled around the slant of her hat. Hugh brought Polly to his side as the welcoming party gathered around to meet his mother.

"Polly, please welcome my mother, Adele Perry. Mother, this is my bride to be, Polly Norcutt." The trio visited briefly before Hugh continued. "Of course, these other folks also want to meet you. This is Dr. Adam, whom you already know, and his wife, Clarissa. Please meet their sons, Nathan, and twins, Wyatt and Warren."

"From Hugh's letters, I feel I already know all of you," she said. "Thank you for such a warm welcome."

As soon as the formalities were over, Adam suggested, "Adele, please take a few moments to get settled over at the Excelsior. We'll send the twins home with Nathan, and the rest of us will wait for you in the hotel dining room. Take your time, but we're all anxious to share Polly and Hugh's excitement. I'll order tea for our table when you join us."

Without lingering, Adele walked away with Hugh. At The Excelsior, Mr. Lawson, the proprietor, ushered them to Adele's room, unlocked the door and opened the drapes to let the beautiful day shine through.

"I hope you'll enjoy your stay with us, Mrs. Perry. We've been looking forward to your visit. Your son has been a wonderful addition to our community."

"Why, thank you. Everyone in Lexington certainly misses him."

After the door shut, Adele removed her travelling gloves and again embraced Hugh.

"Son, it is so good to see you. Life out here in the country certainly agrees with you."

"Yes, it does. I'm so sorry Father isn't here to meet Polly and enjoy this next big step in my life."

"Let me unpack a few things while we visit."

Hugh smiled. "And please unpack Grandmother's ring so I can give to Polly tonight."

"I didn't bring it." She busied herself shaking out her wrinkled clothes.

"But how could you forget it?"

"I didn't forget it. I left it in our safe box. Hugh, darling, you must not marry this girl."

"What?" He took a deep breath. "You're serious?"

"I'm very serious. You need to end this relationship."

"Mother, I know she's not one of those Lexington socialites you picked out for me. But she's wonderful, she's beautiful, and she's the one for me."

"Take my word on this, son. This marriage must not take place."

"This is ridiculous! Why not?"

Adele remained silent and didn't answer his question.

"Come on, what am I supposed to tell Polly? Something like, 'My critical, overbearing mother has changed my mind?'" His face flushed with fury.

Adele looked out the window and didn't reply. Hugh broke the silence.

"I'm not doing this, Mother. You cannot choose the woman I marry. I'm not going to break off my engagement to the woman I love without knowing the reason why. Tell me. I insist."

"Lower your voice, Hugh. Engagements are broken all the time. Just tell her I've revealed some family problems you weren't aware of before. Or think of something else yourself, I don't care. Just stop this engagement now, or I will."

"Then we'll elope. You can't come in here like this and ruin everything for Polly and me. The least you can do is tell me what this is about."

Suddenly Adele stopped taking things out of her case and started throwing them back in. "All right, since you won't be reasonable. If you must know, Hugo Perry is not your father."

Hugo stared at her blankly. "What? What are you talking about? I'm sure my father would deny this."

"Yes, he would because he never knew."

"So, even if it's true, what's the problem? How does it affect my plans with Polly? This is ridiculous."

After a long silence while Adele stared out the window, she said, "Polly is your sister."

"Are you insane? What on earth are you saying?"

"Brothers and sisters are not supposed to marry and have children."

"I know that, but what does that have to do with me?" He paused. "Unless ... Wait a minute. You had an affair with Dr. Norcutt? That's it, isn't it?"

"That's all I'm going to say. You asked for the reason you cannot marry Polly Norcutt and I've told you. Now go out there and tell her you're not marrying her. You don't have to tell her all the details." She shoved a dressing gown into her case and slammed it shut. "And put me on the next train for Lexington."

"Lord, have mercy! Is a secret affair with Father's closest friend what this is all about? Have you no decency?"

"I'm not going into any more details about a frivolous event I barely remember," she said firmly, but she spoke to her luggage. She couldn't bring herself to face him.

"How can you possibly call this frivolous?" He sank into a nearby chair. "Is that what you think of me?"

"Certainly not." Her shoulders sagged and there was a moment of silence. Finally, she turned around, and sat down on the edge of the bed. "Look, it was late, your father was off on an emergency call—as he often was—and we'd had too much to drink. I called it frivolous only because all these years later, I know that it wasn't important. You are my son, and Hugo Perry was your father in every way that matters. But you must break it off with Polly before this goes on any longer."

"What am I supposed to tell her? And her parents?"

"Something simple like, you've decided to call off your engagement. Feel free to blame it on me and family complications. But if you wish to discuss our predicament openly, I'll comply. Ask Adam and his wife to come back here. I should be the first to speak with them about this."

Hugh paused a moment outside Adele's room to collect his thoughts. He had no idea how to break this news to Polly. He struggled with his mother's disclosure and her deception through all these years.

"I guess I might as well get on with it," he muttered as he walked to the dining room where the Norcutts waited. Once there, he plunged right in.

"Folks, unfortunately I've just heard some unsettling news from my mother. If you will join her in her room, she would like to speak with you about it. I'll stay here with Polly and explain to her."

"Of course, Hugh," said Adam as he reached for Clarissa's hand. "But I hope everything is all right?"

"Can't say that it is, but I'll let Mother explain it. Polly, let's take a walk and we'll meet everyone back here."

Her face full of concern, Polly walked with Hugh across the street and over to the shaded square.

"Why don't we sit here where we won't be overheard," said Hugh.

He sat close to her on a park bench, not speaking until Polly nudged him. "Hugh? What on earth did your mother say?"

"Sweet Polly, this won't be easy, but I'll try to explain."

CHAPTER 29

Adele welcomed the Norcutts as she cleared up the clutter from her arrival. Then she gestured them toward chairs and took a seat herself. She seemed reluctant to speak, but after a moment, she began.

"Clarissa, I need to discuss something personal with your husband. You may want to wait outside the room, but you're free to stay."

Puzzled, Clarissa's hand flew to her mouth.

"Well, Clary, stay if Adele wants you to," said Adam.

"Go ahead," she patted Adam's arm. "Whenever Adam has needed another pair of hands at the clinic, I've often helped him. I'll stay, Adele."

"This is nothing of a medical nature, Clarissa."

Struggling to speak, Adele stared into space, then took a deep breath, and looked straight at Adam. "Since our children want to marry, you should know that Hugo isn't Hugh's father."

Trying to appear composed, Adam cleared his throat before speaking. "Adele, Hugo never mentioned this to me."

"I'm not surprised. You were best friends, but there was a side of him you weren't privy to. Hugo protected his reputation at all costs."

"Yes, so what is your concern?" asked Adam.

"Hugo had several affairs that I was aware of. Somehow, I was able to forgive him. On a day to day basis, we were devoted to one another. But there's something else you should know."

"Go on, Adele, but I have only the utmost respect for both you and Hugo."

"Adam...you are Hugh's father."

Speechless, Adam stared at Adele. He stood and turned away from her as he clenched his fists. She started to continue, but he held up a warning hand. Clarissa sat—paralyzed.

"Adele, you've just made an audacious accusation which most certainly is not true." He spoke in an angry whisper. "Why would you say such a thing? How dare you insult me and Hugo like this?"

"Adam, I would never construct such a lie."

"I'm furious that you imply this in front of my wife. You and I never...."

"But it did happen once," she interrupted him. "You were still living in Lexington and came to an open house celebrating our newly redecorated home."

Adam's voice rose. "What? This absolutely did not happen."

"Adam, shhhh," whispered Clarissa.

Adele continued in lower tones. "We'd all had too much to drink. However, to the best of my memory this is what happened."

"I do remember touring your home that night."

"Then, don't you recall that Hugo was called away on a medical emergency? And you stayed to finish your drink? We had several more nightcaps and the unexpected happened...something we never planned or repeated. When Hugo returned, we could tell you were in no shape to walk home, so we loaded you into our carriage. Hugo saw you safely home."

"Go on," said Adam. "But I have no recollection of...anything of this nature."

"During our marriage, Hugo and I were intimate on rare occasions. When I told him I was pregnant, he was overjoyed. But all along, I knew the timing was off for him to be the baby's father. We were thrilled to have a son and Hugo was a devoted father. Hugh has fair coloring like all in our family, but oddly enough, unlike his blue eyes, all of us have brown eyes. Sometimes I retreated into myself with this truth for days. Whenever that happened, Hugo blamed it on birth blues and prescribed a sedative for some relief."

"I'm not sure I can accept this." Adam rubbed his forehead with a shaking hand.

"I knew you would be skeptical," said Adele. "But my concern now is for the future of our children and our grandchildren."

"Why?" asked Adam.

"Well, you deal with similar issues breeding horses, don't you?"

"I'm not sure what you mean. What issue exactly worries you?"

"Well, isn't it obvious? Now that I've told you this, aren't you concerned about a brother and sister marrying? What about the well-being of Hugh and Polly's children?"

"Why would I..."

Clarissa grabbed Adam's arm and whispered in his ear. "She must not know you adopted Polly."

"What don't I know?" asked Adele, who heard part of Clarissa's whisper.

"Adele, I may or may not be Hugh's father. However, I was privileged to become Polly's father when she was just a little girl. Polly's original father has been dead for years." Shocked, Adele glared at Adam. He continued, "Clarissa and I adopted one another's children after we married."

"It never occurred to me...to us, that Polly hadn't told Hugh how our family came together." said Clarissa.

"Both Nathan and Polly were very young when we adopted them. We raised them as siblings," said Adam. "Later we had our twins, Warren and Wyatt, whom you just met."

Adele stared at them. "What a surprise...go on."

"Polly was the first baby I delivered in Springdale. She's always been special to me."

"When Adam brought his six year old son from London, he needed a governess," explained Clarissa. "At that time, I was a very poor widow, so I welcomed the income. I also did his mending and tried to give Nathan piano lessons."

"We helped one another through some difficult times and ended up falling in love," said Adam. "You have no reason to worry."

"Well, that's a relief. You'll never know how much sleep I've lost over this...which isn't an issue after all." Adele looked away and stared out the window. "Adam, I apologize. To think I could've kept this secret, and no one would've ever known. But now I suppose we must all discuss this together."

"These things, true or not, have a way of coming out on their own when least expected," said Adam as he and Clarissa left the room. "Meet us with Polly and Hugh in the dining room for tea when you're ready."

CHAPTER 30

After everyone was seated in a quiet corner of the Excelsior dining room, Adam ordered afternoon tea. An awkward silence prevailed until Polly spoke up.

"So, now that everyone knows about these family issues, what should we do with this information?"

Clarissa reached for Polly's hand and kept silent. Hugh looked at his mother, who never balked at discussing complicated topics. In fact, she delighted in being on one side or another of any controversial issue. This time, she found herself without a cause.

Adam stepped in with a suggestion that put everyone at ease.

"This has been difficult for all of us. We've undergone the scrutiny of a…very private nature. Let's join hands and pray silently for God's grace to join us."

The small circle joined hands and all were silent. After a moment, Adam prayed aloud, "God help us all, Amen."

Hugh spoke first. "I think the main issue we face now is if today's discussions need to become fodder for public debate. I know my mother was honestly speaking up for what she thought was best for all of us."

"That's perfectly clear, Hugh. But should anyone outside this circle be privy to our disclosures to one another?"

"Why does anyone have to know any of this?" said Clarissa. "My situation with Polly is of court record, as is Nathan's with Adam. No one will be expecting any more information unless those of us in this circle choose to divulge it."

"I've certainly kept my information private for many years. I see no reason to expose it now," said Adele with an air of finality.

There was an uncomfortable silence around the table until Adam spoke.

"Let me address one issue that is, in my opinion, uppermost in our concerns. It is my wish that Dr. Hugo Perry be considered Hugh's father, as he always has been. Without Adele's visit today and her very real concerns, no one would've known otherwise. As you know, I'm hesitant to accept her information, but if I must, so be it."

"I'm certainly in favor of that, Dr. Adam," said Hugh. The others, Polly, Adele, and Clarissa, joined him with a slight raise of a hand.

"I truly regret divulging something I thought was going to be devastating to you and Polly in the long run. Now I wish I could take back my words," said Adele.

After a few moments of gentler visiting, Adam suggested, "Unless anyone has other concerns, let's agree together that today's difficult conversations remain sacrosanct."

He looked around the circle as each acknowledged their agreement.

"Now I have a clinic to open. Dr. Hugh, why don't you and Polly go to your apartment and begin to make it your home. Ladies, plan this wedding for as long as you like."

"Folks, Polly and I are officially engaged." Hugh gave Polly a resounding kiss and they rose to leave. "Now we can move forward with our plans."

"But, wait! What do you want for your wedding?" asked Clarissa. "Your mother and I don't even know where to start planning."

"A beautiful wedding at your home before the weather turns cold," announced Hugh.

"And not too fancy," added Polly.

"You two run along. Planning parties is my specialty," said Adele.

On the way out, Polly whispered to Clarissa, "Mamma, may I wear your wedding gown?"

As he left, Adam saluted the women. "Ladies, I'm leaving this wedding in your capable hands. I'll happily host the wedding at our home. And consider this event fully funded, Mrs. Perry."

"Now let's plan a wedding," said Clarissa.

"After a glass of wine," said Adele.

Adam spoke to Hugh as the three walked together across the square to the Springdale Clinic.

"Hugh, I think it would be wise for the two of us to be open about your mother's disclosure today. It may be true or not. Either way, please know it has come as a complete surprise to me. I certainly don't want all this to come between us in the future."

"Let's be open between all of us," said Hugh as he put his arm around Polly. "Honestly, I harbor no hard feelings toward you. In my mind, you are my boss at the Springdale Clinic. In my heart, my father is Hugo Perry."

"Agreed," said Adam. "I'm about to become your father-in-law, and I'm happy to fill that role in your life. Yours as well, Little Girl."

"Thank you, Papa," said Polly.

With Adele's concerns laid to rest, Hugh escorted her to the train station the next day. As they parted, Hugh told her, "Mother, I'm coming next weekend to pick up Polly's ring, if that's not a problem for your busy schedule?"

"Good idea. I don't dare put something that valuable in the post."

"It'll have to be a quick visit because I'll be taking off two weeks for my honeymoon with Polly."

As the train left the station with plans in place for a late summer wedding, Adele breathed a sigh of relief.

"So, my Hugh has two wonderful fathers. Who am I to complain?"

CHAPTER 31

𝒯he few days after their difficult time with Adele at the Excelsior, Clarissa said, "Well, Dr. Norcutt, that explains Dr. Hugh's blue eyes."

Adam reached out for her, but she turned away.

"Stop, Adam. Listen, I've known all along about Nathan's beginnings, and now there's Hugh. How many more of these secret children of yours are out there? I hope some frollop of a woman doesn't waltz in here someday claiming to be your child. Maybe claim a share of your family fortune? Perhaps this farm and its furnishings?"

Adam's lips twitched. "I believe the word you're looking for is 'trollop,' and you don't need to worry about that. Clary, surely you don't suspect such silly possibilities, do you? Years ago, I lived a frivolous lifestyle as a bachelor. I didn't realize how off balance I was. This revelation about Hugh is a complete surprise to me."

"But I'm serious. I need some assurance that our family won't face this on a regular basis. Will these shadow children of yours always be lurking out there? Our four children, the ones we have right here with us now, are enough for me. I hope for you, too?"

"Please, don't worry about something that doesn't exist. Clarissa, don't do this to yourself."

"I'll try, but this fourth son of yours, though a perfectly nice young man, is quite a shock." She wiped away tears and Adam took her handkerchief from her.

As he wiped away a tear she'd missed, he held her close. "I'm aware of your concerns, and I share them. We'll get through this together, but I honestly don't think there are any other shadow children are out there."

"Well, if they are, I hope God is taking care of them somewhere else. Not at Fresh Meadows Farm."

"Sweetheart, I also have a concern. Please promise me you won't take in any more strays." He pointed to her heart. "Homeless and hurting, they seem to find you…and me. We already have quite a menagerie."

Clarissa took her blue wedding gown out of the wardrobe where it was stored. When Polly tried it on, they were surprised that it required very little alteration. Polly's joy was evident as she looked at herself in the oval mirror and spun around in her mother's gown.

But Clarissa was still hesitant. "Are you sure you want to wear my dress? The ladies at my boutique are begging to create a dress for you. We have lovely French silks that could be used in a beautiful gown of your design. So?"

Still wearing Clarissa's blue gown, Polly looked again at her reflection.

"Thank you, Mama. But I still want to wear this one. It matches Hugh's wonderful blue eyes. And it was yours."

Clarissa, barely able to speak, said, "Then, let's pin it up for a perfect fit."

Afterward the fitting, Polly ran out to join Hugh. With the blue wedding gown over her arm, Clarissa looked down at the couple from an upstairs window.

"How could you know?" She whispered and choked back tears.

Years ago, Clarissa had created her unique wedding gown from blue silk brocade because it matched Adam's amazing blue eyes.

One evening, after a lovely supper with the Norcutt family, Hugh and Polly sat close together in the parlor.

"I never thought I'd meet the girl of my dreams outside a railroad depot. And, certainly not a beauty wearing a split skirt on a horse with another man."

"We wanted to impress you with our back country ways. But we were ready to hire a buggy for you if you refused to ride on horseback."

"At first, all I could see was that big horse of Leon's. When Leon finally allowed me to ride Miner Boy, I ended up with those broken ribs. And, I was nursed back to health by you, any man's dream. That's when I fell totally in love with you."

"That's good to know. I guess we can only thank Miner Boy for what we have now," whispered Polly.

"Are you ready to be the wife of a small-town doctor?"

"Of course, I'm ready. Or why would I agree to marry you?"

"If you're so sure, I know I am. So, let's make this official." He reached into his watch pocket. "Polly, will you wear this ring and be my bride for the rest of our lives together?"

"Oh, Hugh, it's lovely. Of course I'll wear it, but a simple band would be enough for me."

"Well, I certainly wouldn't agree to that. Not when I have the ring my grandmother intended for my bride. May I put it on your finger?" She extended her hand and he slipped the ring on her finger. "So, my little bride, let's go out and share this moment with everyone."

"Not yet, Dr. Hugh." The next moments in the parlor were lost to everyone but Hugh and Polly…except for the twins, who watched from the upstairs banister. When they giggled, Hugh looked up and shooed them away.

CHAPTER 32

*O*n the morning of their wedding, Polly and Hugh welcomed a warm summer day with a cloudless blue sky. Flowers cut that morning from gardens all over Springdale soon filled the Fresh Meadows plantation house with their perfume. A host of friends stood by to make certain the special day would go smoothly.

Sophie, Pastor Steven's wife, played the grand piano so Clarissa could enjoy her role as the mother of the bride. Nathan greeted wedding guests at the front door and escorted them to their seats in front of the East windows of the living room.

Even though Polly begged him, Leon refused to wear his Shawnee clothing. Dressed in a new suit, he assisted women from their carriages and up the steps of the veranda. Wearing the pink organdy dress Gisela re-made from the one Polly wore when Clarissa and Adam married, Sunny spun around and around in circles.

Polly and Hugh asked the twins to be their only attendants. As the wedding music began, Warren and Wayne, on their best behavior, entered carrying small pillows holding the gold wedding bands. The guests rose to their feet as Polly came down the stairs in Clarissa's blue dress. She had chosen a small, stylish blue hat from The Ladies' Fashion Boutique to complete her bridal outfit. Trying their best to stand still, the twins stood by the altar as Adam met Polly at the foot of the stairs.

"You'll always be my Little Girl," he whispered as he escorted her to the East windows where Hugh waited.

Pastor Steven performed a flawless marriage ceremony as the couple pledged to be loving partners for the rest of their lives.

Family and friends applauded when Dr. Hugh kissed Mrs. Perry for the first time.

Resting in its place of honor on the dining room table, Magnolia's wedding cake was a sight to behold. A crystal punch bowl full of fruit punch had chilled all night in the cellar. Glowing white candles in sterling candlesticks, platters of cucumber sandwiches, bowls of fresh berries, and slices of melon completed the lavish spread.

Gisela wore a yellow silk gown of her own design. Her long blond hair was loosely braided down her back. Fragrant yellow flowers were plaited into the braid. She served slices of wedding cake to all the guests after Hugh and Polly shared the first piece.

Willy stood in the shadows to inform Magnolia whenever a platter needed her attention. However, his main task was to hold Jethro. As he went back and forth to the kitchen, his son slept through the entire event.

Dr. Hugh had made plans for a two-week honeymoon in Charleston with reservations for a private suite on their overnight train ride. The newlyweds would leave later that afternoon. As the reception wound down, everyone gathered on the veranda to wave goodbye to the newlyweds.

Leon's only dark moment of the day came when he observed Gisela having a long conversation with Mr. Les. Feeling the now familiar wrench in his heart, he muttered, "I know how to stop this." He made his way over to the pair engrossed in a lively visit.

"So glad you could be here, Mr. Les," said Leon, as he took Gisela's elbow. "I'm sorry to interrupt your visit, but Miss Gisela's help is needed elsewhere right now. Please forgive us."

As they walked away from the frustrated haberdasher, Gisela fumed. "Why you do that, Herr Leon?"

"Do what?" He escorted her toward the dining room. "You're neglecting your job."

"I don't have job."

"Yes, you do. You're supposed to serve the wedding cake. Magnolia doesn't want you wandering off like this."

"But look at cake."

Leon stared at the empty cake platter.

"Well, I'm sure the ladies still need your help with the drinks."

"No, Magnolia said when cake gone, I should help Miss Polly. Then enjoy party."

"Mrs. Perry still needs your help getting ready. They're leaving shortly."

"But she tell me she doesn't need my help."

"I'm sure Dr. Hugh doesn't want to be late for that train. Be sure their luggage is ready on time."

"I've done that. Plenty of time before train leave." She jerked her arm out of his grip. "Now! You go check on horses. Guests leave soon. Need buggies. Everyone going outside."

"Now you sound just like that little German mail order bride who wouldn't do what her escort asked."

She grimaced and stomped away. The fragrance of the flowers in her long braid stayed with Leon. He was out of words, but knew when to stop. She was right, he was in charge of the horses and she was in charge of—Gisela.

Family and several good friends waited at the Springdale depot for the bride and groom to arrive. Willy brought several servants along in the buckboard. Gisela sat beside Magnolia to help with Jethro, who screamed all the way into town. Adam and Clarissa rode into town with Adele in a hired rig.

Cheers went up when Leon pulled the decorated Norcutt rig up to the hitching post.

All aglow, Hugh and Polly hurried into the depot. The locomotive waited in clouds of steam as several passengers boarded, found their seats and stowed their luggage. Dr. and Mrs. Perry walked to the end of the train to stand on the outside platform of the caboose and wave farewell to their guests.

When all the good-byes were over and it was time for the Norcutts to return to the farm, Leon turned the decorated buggy over to the Norcutt family. Nathan waved to Leon.

"Thanks for all your help today. We couldn't have managed all that traffic without you. Willy brought Miner Boy into town so you and Gisela would have a ride home."

"Glad to help out."

Leon waved to the Norcutts as they left the depot. Adele retired to the Excelsior and planned to leave for Lexington on a train late that afternoon.

Because of her long dress, Gisela rode sideways behind Leon on Miner Boy on their way back to Fresh Meadows. Sunny, exhausted and covered with smudges of wedding cake, sat quietly between them. Since Leon interrupted Gisela's visit at the reception with Mr. Les, she'd said little to him.

"Need book," said Gisela.

"Book? What book?" Leon asked.

"Word book."

"You mean the one with German and English?"

"Yes."

"That's a dictionary. But it's at home, so you'll have to wait." They rode on in silence until Leon spoke. "You look very pretty today, Gisela. Not at all like that angry little lady I met at the depot. You know, the one screaming at the top of her lungs in German. You were a sight to behold that morning."

"Terrible day. So afraid. Angry at Papa, at escort, at dead Farmer Featherson."

"You're better now. Right?"

"Yes. Today like dream. Never have beautiful dress before. Never go to wedding. No nice party. I do all at your farm."

"It's not my farm, Fraulein."

"No, but place you brought me. Sicher."

"So, little farm girl, do you feel sicher now? Safe?"

"Yes. You kept promise."

After they arrived at the farm and Gisela tucked Sunny into bed, she ran to her room to change out of her yellow dress. She hurried back to find Leon in the barn.

"Now I need book." She stood with her hands on her hips.

"Sorry, I forgot. Why do you need it?"

"Need word."

He brought her the worn dictionary, their lifeline before she learned enough English to communicate. She shuffled through the pages.

"Need some help?" he asked.

"No, I find."

When she pointed to a word and then at him, he looked at her surprised, "Me?"

"Yes, Herr Leon. Handsome for wedding. Gutaussehen."

"Why, thank you." He felt himself blushing.

"And, thank you. Now sicher. Very safe." She reached up onto her toes to hug him. Before he could respond, she ran off into the dark.

"So, you aren't angry anymore?" he called out after her. His open arms fell to his side.

CHAPTER 33

*E*ven though Adele Perry's fears for the health of their future grandchildren were unfounded, now Adam had little doubt that Hugh was his son. Stirred to his core, he struggled with his past lifestyle and behavior. Memories swarmed back to haunt him.

Nathan, Adam's son conceived out of wedlock, lived only because he refused Josephine's demands to surgically end their pregnancy. Instead, he married her. Nathan, always a joy to him, was a constant frustration to Josephine.

What haunted him now? Before his acquaintance with Clarissa and his Christian faith began, his lifestyle was far from celibate.

Clarissa listened to him pour out his heart. "Adam, dear, don't let your past be such a problem. God assures us of His forgiveness."

"Of course, but even with God's forgiveness, I still remember what sort of a man I was in those days. What if I have other children I don't know about? Those that you worried about are now haunting me. Finding out about Hugh has been troubling. To top it all off, I betrayed my best friend, Hugo, by my behavior…if Adele is right."

"But look at your life now. You've helped several orphaned, homeless children both here and at the clinic."

"How so?"

"First of all, you brought Nathan back to America so you two could be a family. His life was a nightmare with Josephine in London."

"Agreed."

"You adopted Polly soon after we married."

"Clary, Nathan and Polly were hardly homeless or abandoned."

"Yes, but Polly most certainly was fatherless. And don't forget about Leon, Sunlight, Gisela, and now Jethro. You've provided a safe place for all these orphans to be raised in. Also, Willy and Magnolia, both orphans as slaves, have a secure home here."

"I guess I hadn't thought of all that."

"Also, Polly and I were penniless when I met you. The first time you paid me for watching Nathan, I went straight to town and bought food. Thanks to you, I slowly paid off all my debts."

"I never knew your needs were so desperate. You always looked so lovely."

"Adam, you don't need to carry this old burden alone. Why don't you talk to Rev. Steven? Maybe a man would understand your dilemma better than I."

The next day, Adam walked to the Trinity Community Church. He timed his visit for school recess and found Rev. Steven standing in the shade as he watched the children play.

"What brings you to our school at this time of day, Doc?"

"I'd like to visit with you and wonder if we might take a ride together sometime soon."

"Of course, it's no secret I enjoy riding anytime. Let's plan on tomorrow afternoon."

The next day, Adam and Rev. Steven followed Prather Boulevard out north of town. They let their horses set their own pace. Promising a shower later that evening, billowing storm clouds hovered over the mountains in the distance.

"So, tell me what's on your mind, Doc? Might as well get right to it."

"Lately, I've been thinking about my past." Adam hesitated a moment before he continued. "As a bachelor, I had numerous relationships with women."

"Oh?"

"Here's the issue. It bothers me that I might have children I don't know about. My son, Nathan, was conceived out of wedlock, but I married his mother to avoid her demands that I surgically end the pregnancy. It occurs to me that there might be others I don't know about."

"Doc, your conscience is working overtime. Let God take care of your past. He's the only one who can take away our sins. He has promised to 'remember our sins no more.' You don't need to be haunted by these old memories."

Adam pulled the brim of his hat over his eyes as a sudden gust of wind brought sharp raindrops their way.

"Better talk later! Our evening shower is coming now. Let's turn around."

"Good idea. I'm already soaked!"

The men took off at a gallop toward town. But Adam reined up and yelled over the storm. "You keep going. I need to go back. I just remembered Gisela took Sunny out to Jacob's farm this afternoon. Luke told her to take whatever she wants from that house. I'll bring them home with me on Fancy."

"I'll come with you."

Before they reached the Feathersons' farms, they saw a thunderous mudslide roaring down the narrow ravine in the distance. Boulders and trees were coming down in the path of a sudden flash flood. The horses turned jittery as the ground trembled with the muddy onslaught headed in their direction.

"This flood's coming from that black storm cloud we saw earlier over the mountains."

"Where do you suppose those girls could be?" shouted Rev. Steven.

"No telling. We'll go on, but Fancy may balk at going much farther."

"Let's move onto higher ground and keep looking."

The men found Gisela and Sunny shivering under a ledge high above Jacob's farm. Adam pulled Gisela behind him onto Fancy. He took out his oil cloth slicker to shelter them from the driving rain. Rev. Steven held onto Sunlight and her terrified kitten. None of them dared move until the roaring flood below them subsided.

As they watched the raging waters full of boulders and debris, Rev. Steven remarked to Adam, "Look at all that mess being washed away. That's what God does to our sins, Doc. He washes them away through the blood of Jesus. They're gone forever when we ask for forgiveness."

"What a relief," said Adam.

"All of us need His cleansing. When God forgives us, He also takes away the grief over our past and replaces it with His peace. We just have to claim it."

Adam started throwing big, ugly rocks into the rushing water and shouted to Rev. Steven, "I'm clearing out my memories. One at a time!"

As the flood rushed by below them, Adam pointed up the valley. "Look up there! Parts of Minetown are coming down!"

They watched as the sign from the old silver mine tumbled by. Pieces of furniture and broken lumber followed.

"Don't people still live up in that village?" asked the pastor.

"I don't think so. It's become a ghost town since the mine up there shut down."

"Danke for coming for us, Herr Doctor," said Gisela. "So scared."

"You can thank Fancy," said Adam. "She was terrified, but she knew I wanted her to keep going."

"You have nice horse," said Gisela. "All nice at farm."

Adam was surprised at the warm feeling that came over him with Gisela's praise. His harsh reservations when she arrived in Springdale now seemed trivial.

As the drenched survivors left the shelter of the cliff, Rev. Steven pointed toward the still rushing water.

"So, Doc, where are those dirty rocks you threw in?"

"Can't see a one. All washed away!"

CHAPTER 34

$\mathcal{T}$he heavy rainstorm and flooding proved disastrous for the shanty dwellers along the big river. Their flimsy homes were no match for the downpour, and the flooded river seeped across the land that had been theirs since Emancipation. When Willy visited them and saw their plight, he hurried back to Fresh Meadows.

"Mr. Doctor! Cain't we he'p them shanty folk? They's just sittin' in the mud by the river. It ain't dryin' out no time soon."

"What if you moved them into our back meadow until they can go back home?"

"That'd be a blessing, Doc. How long can they stay?"

When Adam hesitated, Clarissa spoke up, "As long as they need to."

Within a few days, the shanty folk had set up camp on Fresh Meadows land. The Norcutts provided a few supplies and necessities, but the whole community also helped. The Mercantile donated bags of rice and beans. Clothing and bedding was collected by the saloon. Some old tents, stored under the Town Hall since The War, provided shelter. Leon donated his time to help set up the tents. He took Miner Boy along to entertain the children with rides and tricks.

Adam realized that the shanty folks must have medical needs. He turned to his new son-in-law, just back from his honeymoon. "Dr. Hugh, why don't you go out there and see what those folks need? Willy says he hasn't seen any bad injuries, but I'm still concerned."

"Great idea," said Hugh. "I'll go out later today."

"While you're there, warn them about fires. The last thing we need is a big fire."

Dr. Hugh set up a small medical tent for the shanty folks. He took supplies and bandages out with him every morning. Over a small fire, he usually brewed a big granite kettle full of hot coffee. The Mercantile sent out sweets for the youngsters. Soon everyone looked forward to Dr. Hugh's daily arrival.

"Seems that young man has a tender heart," said Adam. "He's handling those daily visits very well."

"He has your caring concern for people," noted Clarissa. "Just like you when you helped Hugo with casualties during The War."

Adam and Clarissa often noticed how much Hugh was like Adam. He had superior skills as a surgeon and Adam delighted in providing his on-going training. Only on rare occasions did his young partner fall short of Adam's standards.

Once at the shanty clinic, Hugh tried to stem the profuse bleeding from a man's lacerated leg. He was applying a tourniquet when Adam arrived to visit the little clinic out in his meadow.

Adam watched Hugh's struggle and began criticizing him. "Why can't you do this?"

"I thought I was doing an adequate job, sir," said Hugh as he released the tourniquet and stepped away from the injured man.

"No! Don't release the pressure!"

"But you said I was doing it wrong."

"It was better than nothing." Adam moved in and completed the task.

When he looked up, several shanty folk stared, wide eyed, at him. He felt his cheeks burn when he realized he had humiliated Hugh.

"Dr. Hugh, forgive me. In the long run, your tourniquet would've helped. I'm so sorry."

He reached out for Hugh's hand and followed it with an arm around his son-in-law. "I'll never do that again, Dr. Perry," he whispered. "You're my son-in-law. Please, don't let this come between us."

"I understand, but I'm always ready to learn from you."

The raging flash flood missed Fresh Meadows, but kept on its destructive path through the Feathersons' buildings and farmland. Due to the ruin of their livelihood, Lucas Featherson and his family decided to move to California. Joel, Jacob's youngest, would go with them to be raised as their son.

The morning after Luke and his family joined the wagon train headed West, Adam asked Gisela to join him out on the dog trot.

"Yes, sir?" she said, her blue eyes wide open in fear.

"Don't worry, Miss Gisela. There's no problem. Luke Featherson stopped by the clinic before they left for California."

"No more Mr. Luke?"

"That's right, but I think you'll like what Mr. Luke left for you." He handed her a document tied with a string.

"For Herr Leon?"

"No, Gisela, it's yours. See if you can you read it."

Gisela tried to read the paper. "What it say, Herr Doctor? Words too big."

"You were sad when Jacob Featherson never met your train, right?" Adam had to conceal his urge to tease her.

"I thought I be his wife."

"And live on his farm. Right?"

"Yes, sir."

"Since you were supposed to be Jacob's bride, Luke wants you to have this." He pointed to the document in her hand. "It's the title to Jacob's farm."

"What 'title?'"

"Young lady, this paper means Jacob's farm now belongs to you."

"Farm? Me?"

"Yes. Before he left, Mr. Luke took Jacob's scribbled final wishes and told the Springdale bank to put Jacob's land in your name."

"This not right. Herr Luke say take things in house. Not take land."

"Just ask Leon to drive you to the bank this afternoon. The banker is waiting for you with your documents for Jacob's farm."

He laughed out loud when Gisela ran off calling for Leon. "Herr Leon! Go to bank. You take me."

Leon hurried out of the barn with an ornery horse in tow. Adam waited long enough to watch him read Gisela's document. When he looked up, shook the papers and started asking questions, Adam shouted, "Just do what she says."

"But? Gisela owns Jacob's farm?"

"Ask her, Herr Leon."

Gisela Schroeder from Germany just became the legal owner of an American farm.

CHAPTER 35

$\mathcal{W}$hen the barn chores were done in the early morning, Leon turned the horses out into the pasture and finished mucking out the barn. When he was done, he whistled for his stallion.

"Come here, Boy. What do you say we go see what's left of Minetown?" With a day trip in mind, he slipped into the kitchen to pack some food for later.

"I sees what you're up to," Magnolia said from the laundry room. "Be sure and take some corn pone to go along with that ham you tryin' to sneak out with."

"Yes' um. Do you know where Gisela is?"

"She's in here."

Hearing Leon ask for her, Gisela came around the corner of the laundry room where she had been working on mending for Clarissa.

"Guten Morgen, Herr Leon," she said. "You still eat?"

"I've had plenty, but I'm packing food for later on today. Dr. Adam has given me the rest of the day off to go up the trail to see what's left of Minetown. Want to come along?"

"You take me? Sunny go?"

"Bring her along. Miner Boy can handle the three of us."

"I go. Change to riding skirt."

"Bring your shawl. It's probably cooler in Minetown."

The trail winding up to the tiny mining village showed signs of destruction from the flash flood. Often, Leon walked and led

Miner Boy around the rough places. Sunny slept most of the way between them.

When the trio approached the yawning entrance of the deserted silver mine, Gisela looked around and asked, "Where town?"

"This is what I feared. That flash flood washed away the entire town. The buildings were always flimsy."

"What flimsy?"

"Like shanties by river."

Profoundly sad, he stared at what was left of his hometown. The huge iron laundry tubs belonging to Sally, Blue Lark's friend, were all that survived the devastation of the flash flood.

"Fraulein, this is where I grew up. I wanted to show you where I lived as a boy, but it's all gone. My mother and I lived right over here."

"Sad place now," said Gisela.

They walked over to where Blue Lark's shack once stood. Some scattered pieces of it remained, but all the galvanized metal and flimsy furniture was gone. Leon found his mother's iron kettle, but nothing else.

"I'll keep this. She cooked in it every day."

As they stared at the remains of his childhood, he was brought face to face with the loss of his only family home. The sadness he had left up in Minetown for several years now returned full force. He sank onto the boulder that had been the back wall of his home and wept. Gisela sat beside him. She reached out to put her hand on his.

"Sorry all gone for you. I same. Mutter died, never stopped crying. Lost home when father sold me. Still cried."

"So that's why you cried for so long in the depot?" He wiped his eyes with his bandana.

"Yes. Herr Leon, we both lose all. We sad the same."

She wept with him. He rested his arm around her until their sadness retreated.

Sunny came running over to them with something she found.

"Well, look at this!" Leon took the rotten leather pouch and looked inside. He held out two perfect turquoise stones.

"Those very pretty. Mutter's, Herr Leon?"

"Yes, she was a Shawnee princess. Her tribe settled in a mountain meadow high above here. Her father was a mighty chief. He gave her these stones and told her they would keep her safe." He shook his head. "I think they failed her."

"Never see these before. Put stones in bag, Sunny. I'll take home for you," said Gisela.

"Let's eat and go down the mountain," said Leon. "I've seen enough."

They shared the ham and cornbread he had brought along, then cupped their hands to drink from the now clear water trickling down the chalk rocks. Miner Boy came when Leon whistled for him. They paused astride him as they looked one last time at Leon's wasted boyhood home.

"Minetown needed to come down," said Leon.

When you pass through waters, I will be with you." Isaiah 43:2

Part Three

Blessed is he who is kind to the needy.
Proverbs 14:21

CHAPTER 36

fter supper, Adam and Clarissa rode Fancy and Moonlight down the driveway away from Fresh Meadows. He pulled an early fall leaf off a tree branch and handed it to her.

"Chilly weather will be here before we know it, and then it'll be too cold for us to ride around in the evenings. When that happens, I'll be looking forward to a big, roaring fire in our living room. Maybe have a spot of tea to warm my insides," he said. "With you."

"Sounds wonderful." She twirled the red leaf between her fingers. "You know, I've been meaning to ask you something. Why don't you devote more of your time to being our Mayor? You're so full of good ideas."

"People elected me on the promise that I'd do new things. Since bringing in the railroad, I haven't done much about that commitment. I just don't have time."

"Honestly, dear?" a touch of irritation in her voice. "It's a choice you make every day. You love being a doctor, we all know that. But you can make time to do more for Springdale." She rode in silence a few moments. "Now that Hugh is here, why not let him take over some of the load for you?"

"He'd probably like that, but he'd never ask me to move over."

"Of course he won't. Just take an afternoon a week off to be our Mayor. Hugh can handle the clinic. He will be flattered, and you could accomplish so much."

"Must admit that's a fetching idea—like you are."

"So, tell me, Mayor Norcutt. What's the first thing you'd like to do?"

They turned off the driveway onto River Road to enjoy the colorful sunset.

"Hmmm, nothing new, but I'd like to start having our Springdale Festival again."

"I'd like that, too." She straightened in her saddle. "Adam, we— you can still do it this fall. People will enjoy coming out when it's cooler. We can have a big market. Farmers can show off their late summer crops. All their spring animals will be old enough to show for purchase. There can be prizes for their wives' best pickles and jellies. And a cake walk is always fun."

Adam smiled. "Now who's full of ideas?" He shook his head. "I don't know, Clary. We should wait a year. We don't have enough time to plan it, and there's a much bigger issue you don't know about. The city doesn't have the money to pay for it. That event fell by the wayside when Widow Nellie Desmond and her parents, the Murrays, moved to Atlanta. They never really enjoyed the festival, but always underwrote it."

"Don't I remember the Murray family brought their own picnic to the festival? And they brought along their own servants in white coats to serve it?"

"Right, and since I was then at Widow Desmond's beck and call, I had to go along with her family's plans. Nathan hated to sit with the Murrays. He just wanted to run around and play with his friends."

"Sounds like you felt somewhat like Nathan."

"Yes, especially on the night I danced that reel with you and our children."

"Dancing that evening was the first time I'd had fun in years."

When little dusk remained, they turned their horses toward home.

"All right, Clary, out with it. I can tell something's on your mind."

"Why can't we raise the funds for a Fall Festival right here? From the town folks?"

"Clever, but how?"

"Simple—we could sell raffle tickets for things people give to the cause. Aunt Mag can donate cookies. Gisela and I can think of something to make at the boutique. I can offer piano lessons. Perhaps Polly can offer an afternoon of child care. You and

Hugh can donate clinic visits. Leon can offer to trim hooves. The Excelsior might donate a dessert and coffee. The ideas are endless for this sort of civic spirit."

"Maybe you should be our Mayor? Seems you're the one with all the good ideas."

"Just set up your Mayor's sign on a table in the front corner of the Springdale Clinic and watch this happen."

"Yes, ma'am." His blue eyes twinkled as he smiled down at her. "I'll ask Olsen to be my committee head on this project."

"First thing in the morning?"

"Remind me."

As soon as Adam reinstated the Fall Festival, Clarissa's fund-raising idea caught on. People in Springdale joined in the fun of raising money to bring back the Fall Festival. Everyone bought tickets with the hope of winning a special item during the drawing.

Clarissa went through the community asking for donated items. Her first donation was a clinic visit from Adam. Other folk donated whatever prize they could offer. With his reluctant consent, the boutique ladies offered, not a hoof trimming, but a kiss from Leon Jonas.

Tickets sold quickly for a chance on the donated items. Any funds left over after the expenses of the festival would be spent to refurbish the Town Hall.

Farmers and their wives worked on their wares to sell around the town square. Clean clothes and polished boots stood waiting for the big event. Farmers scrubbed their fingernails, and boys and girls took baths the night before the big event.

CHAPTER 37

On a clear, colorful fall morning, all of Springdale showed up bright and early for the opening parade of the Festival. As in the past, Leon led the parade dressed in his Shawnee Indian clothing. Miner Boy, at his stubborn best, almost disrupted the parade. Farmers with their best stock and ladies in open buggies joined the entourage. Older boys and friendly dogs ran after the parade.

Later in the morning, Leon walked alongside Gisela and Aunt Mag until he decided to shop for some supplies he needed for the stables.

"Fraulein, I'll only be gone a few minutes. Be sure and stay close to Aunt Mag so she can help you with words you don't know."

When Leon returned, he found Gisela shopping for hair ribbons. She was trying to chat with a tall man he didn't recognize. Very helpful, the stranger kept advising her about which colors to choose. He held different ribbons up to her face to see which ones he liked best. Aunt Mag was nowhere to be seen.

Leon walked closer. He didn't like the looks of the man dressed in the dirty, rough clothes of a common cowboy. He sported a strange looking black moustache. Even at a distance he smelled of cheap whiskey.

Leon stopped and clenched his fists to keep himself under control.

"God in heaven, he's back! And talking to Gisela! He hasn't changed one bit." Chills rose along his back. "Me neither."

No doubt about it, Claude Featherson stood close to Gisela.

Bitter memories of Claude, Jacob Featherson's son, flooded over Leon. Here stood the man who murdered his beloved Rosalie.

Three years ago, Claude denied the murder and remained silent while Leon almost paid by hanging for Rosalie's death. In the last few moments of the trial, Adam, Nathan, Mr. Tinkerslea, and young Joel Featherson provided the evidence to the court that proved Claude's guilt.

Convicted of rape and the death of Rosalie along with her unborn child, Claude was sent away by stagecoach to serve his sentence at a reform school. Along the way, highway robbers held up the stage, killed all the passengers, but took Claude in. His kind of rage fit their violent gang. Since then, he had been considered armed and dangerous with a $500 reward on his head. Leon and Sheriff Olsen always knew he would return one day to settle his imagined scores.

"Pastor," Leon found Rev. Steven and grabbed his arm in an iron fist. "Fetch Olsen! Get him over here before I take something into my own hands. Hurry!"

When the pastor questioned him, Leon whispered, "Just go. Time for questions later." He shoved the preacher toward the sheriff's office.

While Leon waited in the shadows of a nearby stall, he palmed his razor-sharp Shawnee knife. He never took his eyes off Gisela. His heart pounded with fear for this innocent girl under his protection. She had no way of knowing the identity of this filthy cowboy.

Olsen came running, but Leon signaled him to come quietly. "So, Sheriff," he whispered, "You got my $500?"

"What on earth, Leon? $500? Why you sayin' that?"

"You see who I see?" Leon nodded toward the scruffy cowboy.

"I don't see no one to worry over. What's got you so hot and bothered?" Just in case, he flipped the safety off his pistol.

"He's here, Olsen. He's not getting his filthy hands on another one of my...our Springdale women. If you don't take him down, I will."

"Wait a gol'durn minute! That ain't Claude Featherson, is it?"

"The one and only. I'd know him anywhere, even with that fake handlebar. But you'd better take over. If I get my hands on him, I'll kill him."

"You s'pose I oughta' get some help?"

"Go on. Just hurry."

Olsen went over to Rev. Steven, who waited nearby to watch what might happen.

"Preacher, aren't you still sworn in as a deputy from when Leon was tried?"

"I guess so, Sheriff, but what's up? You look scared to death."

"Just come with me. This is serious. Leon is beside himself."

They walked over to Leon.

"Leon, what's going on?" asked Rev. Steven. "You need to calm down."

"Olsen and I need your help taking down a criminal. You up for the task?"

"Sure, but who're we talking about?"

"Don't you recognize that filthy cowboy talking to Gisela?"

"Can't say I do. Do you?"

"I can smell him better than I can see him. But we've always known he'd be back. Can't believe he's already cozying up to a young lady. Just look at him leaning close to Gisela."

"Hold on, Leon. What's gotten into you? The man's just talking to her, isn't he?"

"Just think of him screaming at Judge Stallcup," said Olsen.

"Or with blood on his hands down by the river," added Leon.

"That's Claude?" The breath whooshed out of Rev. Steven.

"None other," Leon spoke in a rough whisper. "Now, can you help Olsen take him?"

When Olsen pressed a small pistol into Pastor Steven's hand, he pushed it into his belt behind his back.

"He's strong as an ox," said the sheriff. "So, we need to hit him at the same time and push him onto those ribbons. Help me pull his arms back, then I'll put my cuffs on him. If he struggles, I'll hit him in the back of the head with my pistol butt."

"I'll take Gisela out of the way," said Leon.

The duo landed together on Claude, forcing him onto the slippery, colorful ribbons.

"Claude Featherson, I'm taking you to jail for the crimes you committed against Rosalie Featherson. Since you've become a cattle rustler, you are considered armed and dangerous," said Olsen. "There's a reward on your head."

Claude snarled and cursed as he struggled against Olsen and Rev. Steven.

"You're just a no-good, small town excuse for a sheriff." His fake mustache fell to the ground. "You'll regret this, Olsen! I got friends who'll tear up Springdale over this."

"We'll take on any of your gang with pleasure, Claude. Now let's move on over to the jailhouse. I've had your cell ready and waiting for a long time."

The marketplace came to a standstill. No one in Springdale had forgotten when Claude Featherson almost let an innocent Leon hang for the murder of Rosalie Featherson.

Leon tried his best to explain to Gisela what was happening.

"But man nice to me." She challenged his story.

"Ask Aunt Mag to explain this in German. This man killed the woman I loved."

As she took in what she could understand, she patted his shoulder. "Now more sad for you. My heart unhappy for your heart, Herr Leon."

Leon tried to pay the shopkeeper for the damages, but she refused it. Instead she gave Gisela a handful of ribbons.

"Let's go sit on the lawn of the Town Hall until things settle down," said Leon. "I want to be sure Claude goes to jail this time."

They watched as Olsen and Rev. Steven struggled with Claude toward the jailhouse. Fighting against them, the filthy criminal broke loose and ran.

"Halt!" shouted Olsen. "Stop, Claude, or I'll shoot."

Claude never slowed down even though both the sheriff and the pastor warned him again and again. Sheriff Olsen pulled his pistol and fired at the running man. His bullet went through the middle of Claude's back, and the wanted man fell in full stride.

"Stay here, Gisela." Leon rushed over to where Claude lay face down in the dust. He put his hand on the sheriff's shoulder as they looked down at the wanted man. Dr. Hugh, who'd heard the gunshot, rushed out from the clinic and checked on Claude. He shook his head when he felt Claude's pulse.

"You all right, Olsen?" asked Leon.

"I guess so. We gave him plenty of warning, but I've never killed anyone before. I sure wish he'd stopped."

"But he didn't. Plenty of us heard both of you shout at him to stop or you'd shoot."

"Maybe I should've shot over his head?"

"You did what you had to do, my friend. What if Claude had escaped and tried to work his way back into Springdale? I'll wager he would've tried to claim his father's farm. Thank goodness it's legally in Gisela's name now."

With his back turned to the curious onlookers, Dr. Hugh asked, "What shall we do with this man's body? Isn't he a Featherson?"

Pastor Steven spoke up with a solution. "We could bury him in the Featherson family plot, but I doubt Luke would like that. Claude killed their daughter along with her unborn child, and she's buried out there. There's a gravesite in the far corner of our church graveyard that might work. What do you think?" The men staring down at Claude agreed with his solution.

"Well, it's over now," said Olsen. "I just never thought I'd shoot a man in the back. Guess I'll have to learn to live with that."

"We're thankful you brought him down. He would've terrorized this community if he'd run loose on us," said Rev. Steven. "You did your job and did it well." He put his hand on Olsen's shoulder.

"You did your share too, Pastor. I couldn't have brought him down without your help." He shook Leon's hand. "I'll see that you get your reward, Leon. You did the right thing."

"So did you."

CHAPTER 38

On the evening of the Fall Festival before the fiddlers tuned up, the crowd gathered to find out who won the raffle items. Everyone hoped they held a winning ticket for the donations displayed across the front of the stage. The Mercantile haberdasher, Lester Lewis, walked onto the platform, raised his hand and asked for everyone's attention.

"Folks, we've had a wonderful day, but one marred with a sad event this morning. We all regret that a troubled young man lost his life, but we appreciate our sheriff and his deputy, who put themselves at risk to preserve the safety of this community. I've been asked to fill in for the sheriff this evening as we distribute the items to you folks with the winning tickets. But before I begin, I think it would be fitting for us to hold hands and share a moment of silence out of respect for all involved with this morning's misfortune. Please join me."

Lester held up his hand over the silent audience, then prayed, "Lord, tonight we ask that you bless us all as we deal with this sad event in our city. We pray that your peace be very real in our midst. For Christ's sake, Amen." He then added, "Our program will resume in ten minutes."

Allowing for the mood to return to the excitement of the event everyone was waiting for, Lester walked up and down in front of the items on the stage. He held up each one for all to see.

"All right, everyone. Let's get started. Be sure and have your tickets ready as I call out the numbers. If you have the winning ticket, please come forward with it to claim your prize."

Amidst loud cheers, the winners came forward for their items. On purpose, Lester saved one ticket until last. Leon stood in the shadows by the platform to fulfill his commitment of a kiss to the owner of the winning ticket. Lester waved him up onto the stage.

"All right, folks! Here's our last ticket item. Who holds the winning number for a kiss from our own Leon Jonas?" Loud cheers erupted from the crowd, but no one spoke up to claim the kiss.

"Come on! Man or woman?" Laughter lightened the mood, but the cheers slowly faded. Lester repeated the number and said, "Well, Mr. Jonas, if no one claims this ticket, you won't have the privilege of kissing one of our lovely Springdale ladies."

"I guess I'll leave." Relieved, Leon waved to the audience and started down the stairs.

But a small voice from the back of the crowd said, "I have ticket."

"Then come on up here, miss," shouted Lester as he tried to identify the winner in the shadows of the last rows.

Gisela walked up onto the stage toward Leon. He stared at her and shook his head in disbelief. They barely touched in a brief kiss and the crowd applauded. But some hecklers started booing.

"Come on, Leon. We paid for an honest-to-goodness kiss." The clapping increased and took on a loud rhythm. "Kiss her! Kiss her!" Raucous comments continued until Leon waved at the crowd.

"All right, folks! I can do better!"

Smiling, he swept Gisela off her feet in a long, passionate kiss. Her blond hair touched the floor behind her. The crowd applauded and kept on cheering.

Prudence Philips, standing alongside Aunt Mag, said, "Well, would you look at that? He ought'a be ashamed."

"Hush, Pru. He's been sweet on that girl all along."

"You're a fine one to talk. You're making eyes at that Tinker Man all the time."

"That's none of your beeswax. Don't you be saying things about me and Mr. Tinkerslea. He's a gentleman, Miss Busybody."

"Hmpf," muttered Prudence and focused her rapt attention on the stage.

"Herr Leon!" Gisela pretended to be shocked, but leaned into his ear to giggle. "I bought ticket. Maybe you finally kiss me."

"High time, Mrs. Jonas." He pretended to let her slip to the floor.

She grabbed him by the collar and whispered, "Herr Leon! No way to treat wife."

Red-faced, she jumped off the platform and hurried back to Aunt Mag's protection. Prudence Phillips turned her back and looked away.

The next morning, Adam called out as he searched for Leon. "Leon? You out here?"

"Coming, sir. I just put Miner Boy in his stall. I think he has a loose shoe." He hurried toward Adam, who tapped a roll of paper on his on his knuckles.

"What can I do for you, Doc? You sending me to Lexington again? We sure could use some fresh stock around here."

"You're right, but that's not what's on my mind. Let's walk the fence line, so we won't be overheard. We need to talk."

"What's going on? Is there a problem, sir?"

"Sunny has been drawing on things lately."

"Oh, no! Did she draw on something of yours? Or Miss Clarissa's?"

"No, she drew on a paper of yours and showed it to Magnolia."

"Sunlight drew on something of mine? So, what's the problem?"

"This is what Sunny drew on."

Adam handed Leon a piece of stiff paper. Leon took one look at it and fell to his knees. In his hand he held the certificate of his marriage to Gisela Schroder.

"Doc, no one was supposed to know about this. Ever. That's why this document was hidden down in my valise."

"Some charade, Leon."

"No sir! That's not it." He shook the document. "This was the only way I could save Gisela from a life in that filthy saloon."

"How in God's name did you come up with this sordid scheme?"

"No, Doc. Honest! Her no-good father's deal with the broker said if she didn't marry the man who paid her bride price, she automatically became a whore at that filthy saloon."

"That's a flimsy excuse for what you've done, Leon."

"Please, Dr. Norcutt. Look, it's just not that simple. The saloon owner had a deal with that rotten mail order bride company. They're all a bunch of crooks, if you ask me." He looked out into the field a moment while Adam waited for more information. "Look, I found out about her predicament just before the train left loaded with your new horses. This was all I could think of to do. From the beginning it's been a sham marriage. We agreed to never live together as man and wife." He wiped away tears with his red bandana. "What should I do now, Dr. Norcutt?"

"Stop, Leon." Adam put his hand on Leon's shoulder. "No one knows about this. Magnolia could tell this was a document, not just a scrap of paper. But she can't read, so she showed it to Miss Clarissa, who just now brought it to me."

"Gisela will be so upset." Holding his face in his bandana, Leon leaned back against a fence post.

Adam's former resistance to Gisela returned full force.

"My friend, what's been going on all this time? Be honest with me, I mean it."

"Here's what happened, I swear it. After listening to her cry all night, I asked Gisela's escort why all the tears. When that arrogant little vermin told me why she was crying, I was appalled. He began pulling her toward the saloon, and without much thought, I said I'd take her and find a place for her."

"So, you planned all along to bring her here?" asked Adam.

"No, you must believe me, I had no plan."

"Go on. It's hard to believe this all happened so suddenly."

"I agree. But then the marriage broker told me he couldn't release her unless she was married. Doc, when I prayed for a solution, this fake marriage idea just came into my head."

"So, why on earth would she ever agree to this?"

"I honestly don't know. Her father just up and sold her. I had to do something. She was so desperate…just scared half to death."

"So, this," he pointed to the license, "isn't the cover up for some sort of a love affair?"

"No, boss," he tucked his head. "But sometimes we tease. She tells me to be nice to her since she's my wife. We laugh about it-- that sort of thing."

"Then explain your public display of affection at the festival."

"Doc, I swear we'd never kissed until she came up with that winning ticket. God only knows why I agreed to kiss whoever bought that ticket. I'll never live it down. Anyway, after I did my duty for the winning ticket, that crowd cheered me on for an honest to goodness kiss."

"It didn't look to me like you were opposed to kissing her again."

"I guess you're right about that." He grinned and looked into the pasture.

"Leon, you must tell Gisela we know about this."

"It'll be hard to explain this to her. I'll think about it."

"This isn't an option. You must do this."

CHAPTER 39

"Gisela," Leon called from the dog trot where he waited. "Where are you?"

"I help with Jethro, Herr Leon," she shouted from Magnolia's cottage.

"I need you to go with me this afternoon. Sunny is asleep in the laundry room so Magnolia can watch her and Jethro."

"Sorry, can't go." Gisela walked toward Leon with Jethro in her arms. "Magnolia canning fruit. Not safe for baby in kitchen."

"Just ask her. Dr. Norcutt wants me to tell you something important."

"Oh, no!" Gisela took Leon's comment to heart. "He want me to leave? What I do now?"

"Calm down. That's not it." He reached for the baby. "I'll take Jethro to Magnolia. Go put on your riding skirt."

Leon and Gisela rode on Miner Boy to the creek behind the boutique. For several moments, they waded in the cool water.

"Watch me, Fraulein. This is how you do it." He chose smooth stones and showed her how to skip them across the water. He kept putting off the inevitable.

"Why you not tell me important thing?"

"There's no easy way to tell you this, so I'll just come out with it." He turned to look at her, his dark brown eyes into her pale blue eyes.

"Earlier today Sunny took a paper from my valise to draw on. She showed her drawing to Magnolia. And Magnolia showed it to Miss Clarissa."

Hesitating, he tried to think of an easy way to tell her the rest of the story.

"That's good. What picture of?"

"I don't know," said Leon. "Looks like more of her scribbling to me."

"You bring me here to tell me you don't know something?"

"No, Gisela, I do know something. I just don't want to tell you." He turned and walked toward the willow trees. Dragonflies flitted away in his path.

"Then, I go home." She ran toward Miner Boy.

"No, stay," he caught up with her. "It's just, I feel I've betrayed you."

"What means 'betrayed?'"

"I know something that will really upset you."

"Be man, tell me."

"Sunny drew all over this and Dr. and Mrs. Norcutt saw it. So, now we have no secret." He pulled their marriage certificate out of his sleeve.

"Oh, mein Gott, no more sicher?" She grabbed the certificate.

"No! I'll still keep you safe. The Norcutts just want you to know they've seen this."

"What happen now? I leave? I should never trust you at Banhof."

"Please, don't say that. I never wanted anyone to see this document. I hid it in my valise until Sunny took it out to draw on."

"Now old lady with sour face tell all town."

"Miss Prudence doesn't know. Only the Norcutts."

Sobbing, Gisela sat down on a large chalk rock near the stream. Leon paced back and forth. Miner Boy came over and nudged Gisela's shoulder.

"Now big horse worry for me."

Leon reached down for her shoulders and pulled her close to comfort her. Her arms started around his waist.

She shoved him away. "Don't. Not wife." Her tear-stained face shone in the afternoon sun. "I go now." She reached for Miner Boy and pulled herself onto his back.

"Ich bin sauer," she muttered, swiping away her tears. Leon had spent enough time with the German dictionary to know that one: *I am angry.*

The big stallion spun away and galloped along the creek bed in a spray of clear water. Leaning over his neck, Gisela urged him toward River Road.

Leon walked back to Fresh Meadows Farm and knocked on the back door of the main house. His mind whirled with guilt. But nothing he felt compared with his concerns for this girl he'd rescued from a life in hell. Now he questioned why he ever acted on his spontaneous idea to protect Gisela Schroeder.

"What is it, Leon," asked Adam.

"I told her."

"Who? Told what?"

"Gisela. I told her you saw our marriage certificate."

"Well? What was her response?"

"She's furious, feels betrayed. She took off on my horse."

"Where is she now?"

"I have no idea."

"She'll come back, won't she?"

"Probably, but she's afraid you'll send her away."

"How do you feel about this? This plan was your idea in the first place."

"Look, no matter what, I now have a wife who isn't my wife who's run off on my prized stallion." He kicked against the dog trot.

Adam began to laugh. "I'm sorry, but you had to know something like this would happen."

"Yes, but I never thought she'd just leave. I thought she'd end up on another farm or find a husband. When that happened, we'd quietly have our fake marriage annulled."

"But you can't orchestrate everything, can you?"

"Honestly, I've never been in charge of that little lady. I know a lot about horses, but not much about women."

"Does she want to go somewhere else?"

"She ran away from me, not the farm. She feels like Fresh Meadows is a safe place for her. She really likes it here."

"And how do you feel about her being here? I can tell you're attached to one another, for whatever the reason. So, what's your plan now?"

"Sir, I have no plan. My decision was based on what I thought was an answer to my prayer at that train depot. Lately, I haven't worried much about her future. She seems so much a part of Fresh Meadows."

"How so?"

"She does a lot around here. I rely on her help with Sunny. Miss Clarissa depends on her at the dress shop. She helps Magnolia in the kitchen and with Jethro. She was a big help for Polly's wedding. I can afford to pay her under our original plan, so I see no reason to send her away unless she wants to go."

"Let's let this simmer a bit. No need to make a decision now. But you do need to find her."

"Yes, sir."

CHAPTER 40

Leon found Marcus out in the fields walking the beans. The farmer carried a huge armload of weeds he'd pulled out. Leon waved him over to ask his help in searching for Gisela.

"How come she run off? What's gotten into her?" asked Marcus. "You didn't hurt her, did you?"

Leon glared at him. "Of course not. You know I wouldn't hurt her. I just never thought she'd run off like this."

"This sure don't sound like her, least not to me. You sure she's all right?" He quickly saddled up his mare to go with Leon.

"You'll have to trust me on this, Marcus. Nothing bad has happened to her. Maybe she's still getting used to the way we do things here, or something."

"Oh, like buying a chance on that kiss from you? What was that all about?"

"Those ladies at Miss Clarissa's shop twisted my arm to do that. They put a big price on it to raise money for the festival. And they sold one to Gisela."

"So, why'd she buy it?"

"Who knows?"

"Sometimes women do funny things. Sorry she pulled this runaway on you. You gotta be worried about your stallion."

"Right, but I don't think they'll go very far. Miner Boy hasn't had his supper, so he'll want to head home. Let's keep looking."

As the men rode in silence, Leon agonized over betraying his secret with Gisela. Why did this have to happen? Things were going so smoothly until Sunny drew on their document. Before this, the Norcutts had finally accepted their uninvited immigrant. Willy was pleased to have another set of farm worthy hands to help with his chores. Magnolia had taken an instant liking to her. Sunny was devoted to her. This would not have happened if…

His thoughts broke off as Marcus pulled up short.

"Look!" hollered Marcus. "Look what's coming yonder."

Leon stared into the distance. Miner Boy raced toward them at full speed. Gisela leaned forward on his neck with her face buried in his billowing mane. As the horse and rider passed the men, Gisela never looked their way. But Miner Boy glanced at Leon.

"I have no idea what's going on," said Leon. "Let's go home."

With everyone safe at Fresh Meadows, Leon and Sunny went over to Gisela's room to check on her. When he knocked at her door, she sent him away.

"Not talk now."

Then Sunny tried. "I'll see you tomorrow, Sunny. Guten nacht."

"Papa, that means 'good night.'"

"Yes, I know. Let's go to the kitchen and see what's left from supper."

"Shouldn't we take Miss Gisela something to eat?"

"That would be nice. I'm sure Magnolia will find food for all of us."

After they ate their supper, Sunny knocked on Gisela's door with a plate of food for her.

"Miss Gisela, Magnolia fixed you up a plate."

"Danke, Sunny. Just leave by the door."

Gisela was on time the next morning to help Leon feed and groom the horses. Dr. Adam was showing some horses that morning, and he wanted everything in perfect shape for his buyers. The two worked side by side to make sure everything was in order, but they never spoke.

Leon left the barn and returned with tin cups of well water for himself and Gisela. She nodded her thanks, but looked away and maintained her silence. Until Leon spoke up.

"Let me ask you something." He turned her to face him and held her by her shoulders. "Did you like it when I kissed you at the festival?"

Gisela's eyes widened and she tried to jerk away.

"Just answer my question. Why did you buy that ticket?"

She looked away, still silent.

"I want an answer, Gisela. I'm not going to hurt you. Why?"

She whispered, "Didn't think I win."

"And?"

"Thought it be nice if won."

"Nice? Well, was it?"

"First kiss not. Second kiss better."

"So, why didn't you just tell me you wanted me to kiss you?"

"Not right."

"I promise we'll keep our secret. But what if we've come to care for one another?"

Gisela refused to answer.

"You know what? I would've bought a fist full of tickets if you had sold tickets for a kiss. And I would've hoped to win your kiss with every one of them."

"That not right, Herr Leon."

"Why not?"

She looked away, still not willing to talk.

"Listen, Gisela, when we married at that Lexington train station, we never talked about what might happen if we ever fell in love. Like we agreed, I'll keep you safe and keep our secret, but now my heart warms up whenever I'm with you. To be honest, I'm falling in love with you."

"Love? What you tell me?" She glared at him with questions. "Love me like Sunny? Dr. and Mrs.Norcutt? Dr. Hugh and Polly? Miner Boy?"

"None of those--like this." He leaned over to kiss her.

"You kiss better than German boys."

"I'm glad to hear that. Maybe you like me better, too?"

"Maybe."

"So maybe what? Think back to when this started between us in that Lexington depot? What have you thought about me from the beginning? I want to know."

"At Banhof so scared. So lost. Crying and crying under shawl. Saw shiny boots on floor by me. Then you nice. Give me food and water. And chocolate. Then stranger with shiny boots marry me so not go saloon. Must be nice man, I thought. Very nice."

"Well, that's progress."

Just when Leon thought things might be opening up between him and his secret bride, Adam called out from the back door of the house.

"Leon! My buyers just turned into the driveway. Bring our geldings out and tie them up along the paddock fence."

"We go back to work, Herr Leon."

"Yes, we do. Just don't ever run off on my stallion again."

"You not say 'please.'"

"Gisela, I can't always be that horse buyer with his new clothes. I work here, but I'm the same as that man with the shiny boots. I'd like to know you better. Maybe hold your hand? Hear about who you really are?"

"I not talk about that. Maybe you not like."

"Aren't there things about me you'd like to know?"

"You get coffee now."

CHAPTER 41

*M*agnolia kept daily watch over the backyard from her kitchen window. She felt compelled to know the whereabouts of all the Fresh Meadows family and workers. Often, she put a pot of coffee and a plate of leftover biscuits or cake on the table under the trees.

"So's where Leon?" she asked Willy when he came into the kitchen. "How come he ain't come back yet? That coffee mighty cold out yonder by now."

"He and Miss Gisela still talking." Willy stared off into space.

"What you mean? He don't want no coffee? No biscuits? He sick?"

"He tryin' to talk some romance to Miss Gisela."

"He not gonna do that! He's 'posed to find her a rich farmer like that big Jacob Featherson. She ain't interested in no Leon."

"Mags, he's a good man. He mighty nice to her, you know. He brought her here. So, why don't she like him?"

"Never thought of those two like that. But they together all the time."

"Now, tha's what I mean."

They watched an unhappy Leon coming in from the barn for his coffee. Gisela headed in the opposite direction to wake Sunny and dress her for the day. After pouring his coffee, Leon sat down and stared into space.

"Willy, you'd best go talk to him 'bout this," said Magnolia with her elbow in his ribs.

"Why don't you try? Maybe he needs a mama right now?"

Magnolia, never one to back down when someone needed a talkin' to, took some pound cake and went out with Jethro on her hip. When she put the cake in front of Leon, he looked up.

"Thanks, Magnolia. Maybe it'll sweeten me up. Sure not getting anything sweet from that German girl. These days she'll hardly speak to me without getting all bent out of shape." He took a huge bite of pound cake. "She's just so mad at me all the time and mostly I don't even know why. Next thing I know, she can be sweet and happy." He brushed cake crumbs off his chin.

"What you doin' so she go off mad?"

"I have no idea."

"Maybe she just mad all over at men. Any man, not just you. S'pose?"

"I've never heard her mention a man she likes," he paused. "Well, maybe Dr. Norcutt."

"Listen, if a little girl grow up 'round mean type men, she never get over it."

"Gisela left a lot of those back in Germany. But they can't hurt her now. So, why is she upset with me all the time? We've always told her that she's safe here, haven't we?"

"Don't I remember her papa sold her off to marry Farmer Featherson?"

"That's right. I saw the sale papers."

"She not happy in her heart 'bout that. Not never."

"And another thing. Those big brothers of hers never helped her cook or clean up."

"I'll swan! Tha's why she so good in my kitchen. Poor soul had to do my job for a bunch of big orn'ry farmers. She too young to do all that hard work on her own."

Adam called from the paddock. "Leon, I need you out here. You, too, Willy."

Leon tossed out the remains of his cold coffee and trotted toward the barn. "Thanks for listening," he called over his shoulder. "I guess I needed a woman's advice."

"That's what I tol' her," said Willy.

At the kitchen table until the late hours, Leon and Nathan often played Pick-Up-Sticks, a game left over from Nathan's childhood. The two men had never quit playing and arguing. The game became more intense when they grew up and added gaming chips for the winner.

When Sunny saw the set, she begged Leon to let her play. Some nights, they let her join them for a game or two. To their surprise, she often won with her tiny, nimble fingers.

"You're amazing, young lady," said Nathan. "Who knew you could beat the two of us?"

"Papa, can Gisela come play with us?" asked Sunny.

"You can't stay up any later tonight, but you can ask her another time."

One evening Gisela came into the kitchen as the men were playing. "Miss Sunny say I play game with you?"

"Not now, Gisela." Nathan looked up at Leon for support.

"Gisela, Mr. Nathan and I are in the middle of a game. I told Sunny you could play Pick-Up-Sticks with us some evening, but not tonight."

"Big men? You play children's game?" Gisela laughed.

From then on, she often joined in to watch. Finally she challenged Leon by himself and he relented. "All right, but you'd better bring a steady hand."

"I win badminton. Now win this."

On the appointed evening, Leon came to the kitchen table wearing his good boots, freshly polished. He also wore a new shirt made for him by Aunt Mag. He scattered the sticks in the center of the table as he waited for his challenger.

"So you dress up for game? It help you win?" asked Gisela.

"No, I want you to know I'm still the same man I was at the train station. I have some nice clothes, but I don't wear them to work with you in the barn."

"At Banhof thought you rich man with beautiful horses, nice boots, and fancy clothes. Gave me food and chocolate."

"Dr. Norcutt gave me those nice clothes when he sent me to buy horses for him. I'd listened to you cry all night and then scream at that little man. So, I was worried about you."

"But why you nice at Banhof? Crying girl might be bad person." She pointed to herself.

"I wanted to keep you from a life in that saloon."

"How you know about life in saloon?"

"My mother lived her life like that. Only, it wasn't in a saloon, it was worse. It was in our home. No girl will ever be forced into that business if I can stop it."

"That nice, Herr Leon."

"Bringing you here had nothing to do with my boots. You needed a safe place to go."

"Men not nice to me before."

"I'm sure there are nice men in Germany, just none on your farm. Look, I'm strong. I can take care of myself. I work every day around strong horses. One time I killed a mountain lion in self-defense and I made sure Claude was arrested. But I won't use my strength on a woman. If we have a problem, we'll talk it out and find a solution."

"Nice and strong at same time?"

"I hope so. Now, are you ready to play Pick-Up-Sticks? Or are you afraid to lose?"

"I win."

Sunny stood close by to give a chip to the winner of each game. By the end of the evening, Gisela and Leon had almost equal winnings. But Leon won by two.

"Sunny, it's past your bedtime. Run on home and get ready for bed. I'll be there in a few minutes to tuck you in. I want to walk Miss Gisela over to her place."

"Herr Leon, you nice man. Bring me to safe farm and still walk me home?"

"So, maybe you like me better now?"

"Maybe."

At Gisela's door, after a moment of awkward silence, she whispered her thanks again.

"Good night, Herr Leon. I like game with you. Fun, not work."

"You know, in this country a gentleman gives a lady a good night kiss when he walks her to her door. Would that be all right with you tonight?"

"Yes." She leaned in to kiss him and lingered in his arms. "Good night, nice man."

Smiling, he walked back to his cabin. "Who knew Pick-Up-Sticks would help? Magnolia will be proud of me."

CHAPTER 42

$\mathcal{A}$s the farm workers finished breakfast under the trees, Nathan came looking for Leon.

"Leon, Pop wants me to deliver those geldings he sold over to their new owner. I can do it on my own, but don't want to take any chances with those expensive horses. You want to come along?"

"Sure. I'm finished in the barn. Just let me tell Willy I'm going with you."

"I'll bring the horses out front and wait for you."

The men rode along with their delivery well under control. Taking advantage of the moment, Nathan asked Leon about something he'd had on his mind for several days.

"What's going on between you and Gisela? You want to tell me?"

"She does her job and I do mine."

"That's not what I mean, my friend. Look, we've known each other since we grew up around here. You can't keep a secret from me. So, tell me before I ask Pop."

The friends rode in silence a few moments.

"Well?" pushed Nathan.

"I agreed to find her a safe place to live. We've become friends. She helps with Sunny."

"I know all that, but you sort of brighten up around her. She does the same around you. So, what am I seeing? Talk to me."

Leon was silent.

"Look, I know you two played Pick-up Sticks the other night. What was that all about?"

"She's been begging me to play with her. So we did, that's all."

"I'll bet she won! Right?"

"Some, but I went home with two more chips."

"Nothing more?"

"Sure, so why all the questions?"

"I'll tell you why. I saw you kiss her last night. And it wasn't just a little kiss on the cheek. So, tell me what's going on."

Leon groaned and pulled his hat down over his brow. He nudged the horses into a faster pace. "We'll talk more on the way home."

"All right. But I'm holding you to that."

As soon as the horses were delivered, the men enjoyed a delicious noon meal at the buyer's home. Nathan lingered to visit, but Leon took off.

"Sir," Nathan finally interrupted their conversation. "I'm sorry, but I have a pressing obligation back at Fresh Meadows. I'm glad you're pleased with your new horses. Please let us know if you have needs in the future."

"Be sure to give my greetings to your father."

"Yes, sir, I will. Much obliged."

Nathan raced to catch up with Leon. But Fancy was no match for Miner Boy. When Nathan reached home, Leon had vanished.

Later that afternoon, Nathan confronted him. "I know why you left in such a hurry. I'm relentless. You still have an agreement to talk to me."

"I know, Master Nathan. Later, maybe tomorrow?"

"No later than tomorrow after breakfast. And, no Gisela listening in."

Leon grimaced and walked toward the barn.

"Leon?" Nathan called out the next day when he went into the barn. He sat on a hay bale and waited for Leon. Rays of dusty sunshine floated through the silence.

Leon called out to him. "Up here, Nathan."

"You coming down or do I have to come up there?"

"I'll be down directly."

"Then, I'm coming up." With swift steps up the ladder, Nathan stood in front of Leon. "What is this, man? This isn't like you. Why won't you talk to me about Gisela?"

Straddling a rafter, Leon sat in the shadows. "Have a seat."

Nathan found a seat on a three legged stool. "You have something going on with this German girl, don't you? What are you not telling us?"

"Nothing."

"All I want to know is why you two were kissing the other night?"

Leon kicked at the barn pole next to him. "You weren't supposed to see that. It's never happened before. Well, except for that ticket thing she won at the fair."

"That thing, if that's what it was, was close to spectacular. So?"

"Look, I think maybe we've started to care for each other. Any problems with that?" He grinned and chewed on a hay straw.

"I asked you the day you arrived here with her if you were going to marry her. So, why not propose? She came over here to marry an American, didn't she?"

"It was just a kiss, Nathan. Don't make so much of it."

"I think you two would be a great match. She looked beautiful at Polly's wedding in that yellow dress with all that blonde hair braided down her back."

"I know."

"So? She enjoys your company and your horses. Sunny needs a mother. Or maybe you aren't over losing Rosalie yet?"

"No, that's not it." Leon looked away. He knew Nathan was on the right track, but didn't have the right information.

"Well, what's holding you back? Sunny loves her. You need to get married and have a home. She's a wonderful girl. So?"

"I'm married."

"Well, just in case you'd like to tell me, who's the lucky girl?" Nathan waited.

"Gisela."

Nathan threw his stool across the hay loft and left.

171

Nathan rushed in to the Springdale Clinic where he found Dr. Adam seated at his desk. Out of breath, Nathan stood speechless until Adam stood and reached for his shoulder.

"Son? What's wrong? You look like you're about to pass out."

"In shock. Out of breath."

"Shock? Why? Wait a minute. How'd you get here?"

"Ran." Nathan leaned over with his hands on his knees.

"No wonder you're out of breath. Tell me why you're in shock."

"Talked to Leon. Told me he's married. To Gisela." He still gasped for breath. "Pop, what sort of fools does he take us for?"

"Calm down, son. Yes, it's true. Your mother and I found out about this by accident. We've seen their marriage document. I'm surprised he told you."

"This morning I confronted him about Gisela. We all know they're sweet on each other. I kept pressing him to just marry her until he told me he couldn't because he's already married. To her."

"Son, it's a fake marriage."

"That's not possible."

For the next few minutes, Adam tried to explain how Leon could marry Gisela, but not have a marriage.

"When Leon heard about the deal her father made with that German bride company, he was appalled. According to their contract, if a groom fails to claim the bride she goes to a local saloon to be a prostitute."

"But that's horrible!"

"Exactly, and that's why Leon said he would take her. Then, the broker said he had to marry her to claim her."

"So, Leon did a really good thing, didn't he?"

"Yes, he did. And now he's entangled in ways he never planned. Seems to me most days he enjoys being trapped."

"I guess I owe him an apology."

That evening at dusk, Nathan found Leon in the kitchen helping Magnolia clean up after supper. When Leon saw Nathan, he picked up Sunny and walked out. He headed toward his cabin to avoid any contact with Nathan.

"Hold up, Leon," Nathan shouted as he followed him outside.

"I thought you were done with me," Leon said without looking at Nathan.

"Not yet. Slow down so I can tell you something."

"Meet me on the dogtrot after Sunny goes to bed."

When they sat later on the dogtrot, Nathan offered his hand to Leon. Leon shook it, but knew there was more to this meeting.

"What's on your mind now?"

"I was in the wrong this morning when I walked out on you. I thought you'd made fools of us to cover some immoral scheme of yours with Gisela. My father explained your situation, and I want to apologize. Now I understand that you did an amazing thing to help that poor girl."

"Well, at least now you know what's been going on."

"But you never thought you'd fall in love with her, did you?"

Leon shook his head and stared into the rising full moon. "Not a chance."

"I'll make you a proposition. I'm going to Harvard soon. You talk Gisela into marrying you or I'll try to win her heart over when I get back. Fair?"

"What?"

"You heard me." Once again, Nathan held out his hand. "Deal?"

"Why not? But this is no game, my friend. Understand? She's a very special girl."

"I know that, Leon."

"Now that the lines are drawn, plan to stand up with me when Gisela and I marry."

"You mean soon?"

"I sure hope so, but down inside she's still so scared."

"Challenge accepted."

CHAPTER 43

*M*arcus pounded on Leon's door early the next morning. When Leon didn't answer, he rushed over to the kitchen where he found Leon pouring his first cup of coffee.

"Don't even think about that coffee," said Marcus. "Those geldings of yours got out and are ruining my vegetables. Plessie is beside herself because they've already destroyed her plants and flowers."

"But how'd they get out?" asked Leon as he tossed his coffee into the sink. Marcus hid his anger and didn't answer.

"Ya'll go on. I got Sunny," said Magnolia. "And here, you're gonna need these." She handed the men a fistful of biscuits.

The men ran out, but Leon headed into the barn.

"I need to grab some tack to help me bring those horses back. I'll ride Miner Boy over to your place. We'll take care of this."

Rushing to where Marcus stood, Leon saw the broken, twisted wires where the geldings escaped the small pasture they'd been secured in overnight. Because three of the group had been sold, only four horses remained of the ones Leon brought by rail from Lexington. When startled from their grazing on Marcus's vegetables, they scattered in different directions.

Leon slid off Miner Boy and tossed two ropes to Marcus. Between the two of them, they were able to control three of the horses. The other one, the black with a white blaze, took off toward the north. He trampled rows of corn and beans as he rushed around in his panic.

"Let's take these three back to the paddock, then I'll go out for that last one. He can't go far because that pasture is fenced on the back side," said Leon. "I can't for the life of me figure out how they got through that fence. I'll have to repair it later today. Apologies to Plessie."

"Those flowers were her pride and joy." Marcus shook his head and headed back to help his wife recover the pitiful remains of the morning's assault on her flowers.

After Leon secured the geldings in the paddock, he returned to the kitchen for the cup of coffee he'd missed earlier. As he sat at the kitchen table, Gisela called from the back yard.

"Herr Leon, I have horse."

Gisela stood under the big tree in the back yard with the remaining runaway. The exhausted horse's head hung loose in the halter she'd devised to control him. His sides still heaved from trampling over Marcus' vegetables and Plessie's flowers.

"But this horse was running wild," said Leon. "How'd you catch him?"

"I saw him run away from you. When I call, he come."

"Wait? He came when you called him?"

"Yes, he my favorite one you bought in Lexington. I first saw him on train. I call him Herr Schwarz. I give him sugar cubes, so he like me."

"Do you give sugar cubes to all my horses?"

"No, only Herr Schwarz."

Magnolia rolled her eyes. "So tha's why my silver suga' bowl always empty."

After Herr Schwarz was secured with the other runaways, Gisela motioned to Leon.

"Sit here." She sat on hay bales and waited for him to join her. "We talk."

"Of course, what's on your mind? Are you all right?"

"Yes, but Miss Clarissa says you like my idea. So I tell you."

"I'm sure I will agree with whatever Mrs. Norcutt says. Go on."

"Farmer Featherson' farm now my farm?"

"Yes, that place is all yours."

"Can't move to farm just me. Be alone and scared. Not safe."

"But you can hire folk to work and live there. They'll take care of you. You'll be safe."

She stared at the barn floor, hesitant. "Not all Miss Clarissa say to tell you."

Leon took her hand. "So, what's this idea?"

"You and Sunny move to my farm. Then I sicher."

The implications of Gisela's idea landed in Leon's heart. Trying to stop the whirlwind of emotions in his chest, he said nothing. When her tears fell down on their hands, he pulled her chin up to look at him.

"Are you proposing to me?"

"Don't know word."

"Are you asking me to marry you? No more secret?"

"No, Herr Leon. Always keep secret same. Just move to farm so I be sicher there. Safe."

"Then, here's my answer. I won't move in out there with you unless we're together as Mr. and Mrs. Jonas."

"You promised. You always have own place. Not live together."

"Everything's changed because I've fallen in love with you. I can't live out there with you without being your husband. I'll make you a new promise, Gisela. We'll be married and live as man and wife. We'll wear our wedding rings."

"We tell secret?"

"Not unless you want to. That secret was a way to protect you. It's yours to tell or not."

He pulled her to him and dried her tears with his bandana. She leaned toward him as she thought about his plan.

"Don't know how to be married, Herr Leon. Family here nice all time. Not like family on farm in Germany."

"You and I didn't grow up in homes like Fresh Meadows. But we'll figure it out together. I'll always love you and keep you safe. I promise to be kind to you."

"Maybe your idea more better than mine. Maybe."

"Good, I'm glad to hear that. And, think about this. We'll have a real wedding in the church. You can wear a beautiful wedding dress you make at the Ladies Fashion Boutique. We'll walk down the aisle while Miss Clarissa plays the piano. Rev. Steven can hear our real marriage vows. We can have wedding cake and celebrate. So?"

When she jumped up and twirled around several times, he knew her answer was, "Yes!" He caught her and they danced until he stopped to kiss her.

"I be your real wife, Herr Leon. No secret. You always nice man."

"So, does that mean you love me?"

As she leaned into him, she whispered, "Yes!"

They sat in the barn and discussed what to do next. All they could talk about was their future together on Gisela's farm.

"Should we go inside and tell Magnolia and Willie? Or the Norcutts?" she asked.

"Honestly, Gisela, I wasn't expecting anything good to happen today after that disaster over at Marcus' place. You certainly surprised me."

"You think your friend, Farmer Featherson, like our plans? He was good man, yes?"

"Jacob was a very good man and he'd be pleased we've taken good care of you. In his last wishes, he wrote that he wanted to provide for his wife in case he died. That woman should've been you, and that's why Luke signed his brother's farm over to you. Also, I'm sure Blue Lark is happy that I helped the woman I would marry escape life in that saloon."

"Lots to plan now."

"Yes. And, I promise we'll do whatever you wish out on your beautiful farm. We'll raise our family there. That flood didn't take everything away, just what needed clearing out. As soon as we redirect that stream to prevent more flooding, all the good is still there for us to enjoy."

"I still need creek water for crops and flowers."

"You're right, Farmer Gisela. We'll plant whatever you want next Spring and pray that God will bless our efforts. We need to buy work horses."

"...and chickens and rabbits and sheep."

"Sheep?"

"I spin wool and knit clothes for family."

"Is there anything you can't do?"

"Not sure yet. But try!"

CHAPTER 44

The future Mr. and Mrs. Jonas couldn't contain their plans. The secret they had protected for so many months faded into the background as the Fresh Meadows family celebrated their happy news. Gisela asked an ecstatic Polly to be her matron of honor. Nathan didn't hesitate to hold Leon to their past bargain.

"Since you've persuaded Gisela to marry you, I guess I've lost out. Am I standing up with you, or not?"

"In all this wedding excitement, I forgot about our handshake. Of course I want you to stand up with me. You've been with me since I first came down from Minetown. So? Will you be my best man?"

"Deal! No place I'd rather be."

"I need your help with something? How do I plan a honeymoon? I don't have the money to go anywhere. We can't just go home to my cabin with Sunny underfoot. That's no honeymoon."

"Don't worry, Leon. Just leave it all to me. Relax, and look forward to a wonderful honeymoon with that sweet Gisela."

But Nathan had no idea how to plan a honeymoon for his friend. He sat one morning on the veranda trying to think of somewhere the newlyweds could go. Uppermost in his mind was the cost of anywhere Leon could afford.

Clarissa finished in the kitchen and came outside to enjoy the morning sun with Nathan.

"So, Leon has asked you to be his best man? What an honor."

"Yes, it is, but I also agreed to find them a place for their honeymoon. He's at a loss to find a place he can afford. We could put them up at the Excelsior, but that place holds some bad memories for him. As a runaway, he used to beg for food outside the back-door, and later he did other small jobs there."

"Oh, that's terrible. You're right. They need to go to a place with good memories. Surely there's something we can come up with."

"Let me know if you think of anything."

Several days later, Nathan ran up to Clarissa. "I think I've come up with a great solution for Leon's honeymoon. And it's almost free, if we're willing to work on it!"

"I hope your idea works, because I haven't thought of a thing."

"Come with me. Aunt Mag told me what she ran across in Mr. Tinkerslea's wares. I was supposed to tell Leon about it, but forgot about it until trying to plan his honeymoon."

"How can Aunt Mag possibly have a solution?"

"It's perfect. You'll see."

Nathan was right about Aunt Mag's solution. A team of several volunteers went to work in secret to make a honeymoon destination Leon would've never dreamed of. And will never forget.

Even though Gisela and Leon still had the cheap wedding rings they'd never worn, Clarissa decided to offer Leon the solid gold rings from her difficult marriage to his father, Rev. Elliot Chambers. Only Adam, Clarissa and Leon knew that Rev. Chambers had supported a secret second family in Minetown. Leon was the reverend's son with Blue Lark, a Shawnee princess.

"I'm not sure if you want to wear them, but I still have the gold rings from my difficult marriage to your father. If you want them, they're yours," said Clarissa.

"Why don't we let this be the last chapter in my father's sad story? Now he's just a shadow in my memory. Gisela and I will wear these with pride because you gave them to us."

"These rings will now celebrate a new chapter in the life of the son Elliot Chambers barely knew. Any father would be proud of you, Leon."

Gisela agreed with Leon to wear the rings.

"My heart's full again, Fraulein," whispered Leon.

On a day full of fall sunshine, Leon took Gisela out to assess the possibilities of living at her farm.

"Well, what do you think?" Leon asked Gisela as they looked over the wrecked property.

"Not like old mud everywhere."

"If it only needs cleaning, we can easily take care of that. Other things may take longer. But it'll be our house from the beginning of our real marriage."

Later that week they took Willy out to the farm to see what needed to be done. Aunt Mag came along to help Gisela explore the inside of the home. As they looked around she taught Gisela the names of American kitchen utensils.

Mud left behind from the flood still covered the floors throughout the farmhouse. Odds and ends lay scattered on the kitchen table. Other items landed on the floor during the flood. The women found a few utensils in a storage bin, but they could tell that Jacob hadn't kept up the kitchen as his late wife, Merle, would've liked. The mess wasn't all the result of the flood.

"Young lady, you've got a big job ahead. But I'll help and we'll get it done."

Outside, Leon and Willy sat under the huge oak tree that remained after the onslaught of the flash flood.

"Amazing how that rushing water took Luke's farm away and left Jacob's standing, isn't it?" Leon wiped his face with his red bandana. "We'll have to clean up the mud, but the buildings seem intact."

"I 'members when that Featherson bunch bought this land. Master Luke and Master Jacob were barely outta knickers. They was always gettin' licks for something they did bad."

"I imagine they could really stir things up."

"Right about that. But their family was always good people. After us slaves was freed up, I barely had two cents to my name. One day when Mr. Jacob saw me sittin' by the Springdale Stables looking hungry, he hired me on. For almost a year, I hep'd him build these places here."

"And didn't I hear that you helped Dr. Norcutt restore that big house where they live now? He told me you knew all the right men to make the repairs."

"Yes, he did. Paid us well, too. Then he hired me to run the place. I'm a blessed man."

"So, could you come up with a crew to help us with this place? Gisela and I can do it, but it will take the two of us forever."

"Let me see who I can round up. I can probably get a crew…if you pays us."

"Of course, we'll pay you. Let me know when you can start."

"First, let me see if Mr. Doctor will let me off early so's we can come out before dark."

True to his word, Willy found a willing team to clean up Gisela's farm. They found the structure of house in better shape than they expected. They pulled out the parts broken by the onslaught of the powerful flood and ripped out whatever was molded or ruined by the muddy water. They put some things outside to dry for future use. Within two weeks, the old farmhouse began to look like it did in former days.

"Come look," Gisela called out to Leon from the front railing of the porch when he rode up on Miner Boy. "Our house is almost clean again. You like?"

"This is amazing." He wandered through the kitchen. "I have another idea to tell you about. We've redirected that creek that flooded, but I think we can still run a pipe near our back door. That way, we won't have to dig a well or draw water with a bucket."

"You smart man, my Herr Leon."

He wandered around the inside of their home and opened the pie safe and the kitchen cabinet. "We can fill this with some other items you'll need, but that will have to wait. Do you think you can cook with what's here now?"

"I try. Magnolia say she teach me to cook better. She say put a pinch of sugar in everything to lift it. I never hear such a thing."

"If you do what Magnolia tells you, I'm sure we'll be very well fed."

"Don't forget to bring me your mother's kettle for kitchen."

CHAPTER 45

The news of Leon and Gisela's wedding plans spread all over Springdale. Now everyone wanted to know all about Leon's Shawnee heritage and Gisela's strange mail order plans with Jacob Featherson. The fact that Leon rescued her in the Lexington station as she waited for Jacob was discussed over and over again. If Leon weren't a Springdale hero before, he became one overnight. To fold romance and marriage into the horrific story of Gisela's father's arrangement to sell her to a bride company consumed most conversations.

Within the tight circle of people who knew about their original fake marriage, an ironclad pledge was initiated. No one else would ever know about the fake Mr. and Mrs. Jonas of the past. The date on their old marriage document was the only evidence that remained.

There was one exception to this pledge. Leon had to tell Rev. Steven that he and Gisela were already married. The pastor would expect to sign a marriage certificate on the day of the wedding, but there was nothing to sign.

"Leon? What have we here?" asked Rev. Steven when Leon showed him the old marriage paperwork. "You're telling me you're already married to this girl?"

"Yes, it was the only way I could keep her from living in a saloon as...a nightly entertainer. Of men."

"And no one knows about this?"

"Only the Norcutts and Nathan."

The reverend looked over the document in detail and asked, "Didn't you tell me when Gisela attended my school that she was probably 14 or 15?"

"That's what that marriage broker told me."

"According to where she signed her birth date, she's 18." He pointed to the date Gisela had written in German. "Look."

"I can't read German, so I never checked."

After the pastor understood their secret nuptials and the reason Leon and Gisela wanted a new wedding, he said, "Leon, you couldn't have dreamed up this scheme unless God was in it."

"You're right about that. It wouldn't have occurred to me either. But when I prayed and begged God for some way to keep Gisela out of that saloon, this idea came to mind. This solution worked until Gisela and I fell in love. Now we want a real marriage at the church. I'll admit it took a while to convince Dr. Norcutt that we weren't having an affair."

"Everyone will probably assume the same if this fake marriage of yours ever comes to light. The resulting gossip would taint the rest of your lives as a married couple. I promise to file this in the back of my mind under ministerial confidences."

"Now that Gisela's farmhouse is cleaned up enough to live in, we want to spend the rest of our lives there as Mr. and Mrs. Jonas."

"By the way, do you have a name for that farm yet?"

"We're calling it 'New Creek Farm,' but I haven't made a sign yet."

For days Gisela was consumed with creating her wedding dress. Because she and Leon planned an afternoon wedding at the Trinity Community Church, she didn't want a long, formal gown. Instead she chose a soft blue faille to make a long skirt, one that she could shorten and wear later. Her bodice of imported silk batiste was more elaborate. The ladies at the boutique helped her shape it with tiny tucks that emphasized her small waistline. Large puffed sleeves of fine lace narrowed at her elbows and tightened down to her wrists. The ladies made a basketful of tiny covered buttons to fasten the bodice and the sleeves. One of the older ladies crocheted a pair of white string gloves. Clarissa designed a white, wide-brimmed straw hat that held a simple veil and trailed curling ribbons.

Everyone felt relief when Gisela gave her approval. "It's perfect. Now hang it where Leon won't see it."

Leon and Gisela argued over her request for his wedding attire.

"No, Gisela, I'm not doing that. I'll buy a proper suit at The Mercantile for our wedding."

"But please, please wear the beautiful Shawnee clothes your mother made!"

"People will just laugh at me. Anyway, I want them to be looking at you."

He finally conceded. "I'll agree, but only because I want to make you happy, Fraulein."

"I never be this happy before. Ever."

CHAPTER 46

$\mathcal{A}$ fall afternoon set the stage for the bona fide wedding of Mr. and Mrs. Jonas. The large pair of brass candlesticks used by the church for special occasions stood polished and outfitted with long white tapers. With Nathan's help, Wayne and Warren lit the candles.

When the church was packed and people stood around the back, Clarissa began playing the wedding music. The twins now sat with their father, who threatened them with no wedding cake if they misbehaved. Sunny sat with Aunt Mag and played with some small toys she found in Aunt Mag's pocket. Nathan stood at the front facing Polly as they waited for the bride and groom.

When Clarissa began playing the familiar wedding march, Leon and Gisela walked down the aisle together to say their wedding vows. Everyone stood as they watched the tall Indian in his Shawnee regalia come down the aisle with his mail order bride in her lovely wedding dress.

At the end of the simple ceremony, Rev. Steven asked, "Do you both promise to honor these vows for a lifetime together?"

Both Leon and Gisela answered an emphatic, "Yes, I do."

"Leon, you may kiss your wife."

After the guests congratulated the newlyweds and enjoyed Magnolia's wedding cake, Leon and Gisela rushed hand in hand out of the church hall to see what would happen next.

"Come on, Nathan," said Leon. "We have no idea what to do next. What's up your sleeve?"

"Don't worry. Didn't I tell you I'd take care of it?"

"What now, Master Nathan?" asked Gisela. "We go somewhere, but you not tell us?"

"My idea won't disappoint you. Just say goodbye to everyone before you get in the buggy. I've already taken your luggage to your destination. I hope you remember I told you this wasn't a formal place?"

"So you take us? We like your plans?" Gisela still had questions about this honeymoon.

"You won't be disappointed. Let's go!"

Fancy waited with the rig to take the couple to their honeymoon destination. Nathan ran ahead as Leon and Gisela followed under a shower of rice and well-wishes. Gisela paused long enough to throw her bouquet straight at Sunny. The excited little girl caught it and chased after the buggy.

"So, Mr. and Mrs. Jonas, off we go! I wanted to use Miner Boy to take you on your honeymoon, but he didn't like the idea of pulling a buggy."

"That doesn't surprise me. So, let's get going to wherever you're taking us," said Leon.

Nathan eased the buggy onto the road in front of the Trinity Community Church. The newlyweds snuggled in the back seat until Nathan stopped to open the gate at Fresh Meadows.

"Wait a minute, Nathan," shouted Leon. "You're bringing us home? Here? Is this your idea of a joke?"

"Not at all, just be patient."

For several minutes he guided the rig along the rough farm pathway leading north of the barn. When he came to a smaller lane, he stopped Fancy.

"This is where I leave you. Fancy and I are heading back to the barn."

In a flash of memory, Leon grabbed his best man by the sleeve. "I know now where you're sending us. But there's no place to stay out there. This better not be a big prank."

"Trust me, you can thank me later. Take this lantern and go. Miner Boy will be loose down in the pasture, so whistle for him when you're ready to come home."

Leon helped his bride down from the buggy and rushed her toward a place few people knew about. "There's a lake out here. Nathan knows I love this place,"

"Not sure I like! We go home?"

"Look ahead, Gisela. I see some lights. Not much farther."

Torches now lit the way for them to follow. Leon held her hand and pulled her along the path. As they came out of the woods, they were awestruck. On the shore of the lake stood a beautiful white teepee. Glowing from a warm fire within, it looked magical and welcoming.

"How on earth did Nathan do this?" whispered Leon. "Where did he find this?"

"So, we be happy here, Herr Leon? I like?" She drew back. "We be safe here? Sicher?"

"Of course, this lake is off the back pasture and very safe. You've just never seen it before. I promised you wouldn't have to live in a teepee, but I hope you'll let me break my promise. I have no idea how Nathan made this happen. It's like a miracle."

He raised the flap and they went in. The white teepee was identical to the ones Leon had seen when he visited Blue Lark's Shawnee tribe. A low fire burned in the center and smoke spiraled up through the opening at the top. On comfortable benches around the sides, large baskets waited with their clothing and warm quilts. Plenty of split firewood stood ready to replenish the fire. Magnolia had sent along an abundance of food.

Happy to begin their life together, their honeymoon was all Mr. and Mrs. Jonas had dreamed of. They spent long hours wrapped in one another's arms and sharing their dreams. They laughed often, and ate or slept whenever they felt like it. They collected fall berries to eat with the cottage cheese they found in one of Magnolia's baskets. Leon taught his bride to fish with poles Nathan had provided, and they roasted the fresh fish over the fire. He brought clear lake water inside to warm by the fire, but one time he challenged her.

"Come on! We're going for a quick dip in the lake."

When Gisela screamed and refused, he grabbed her in his arms and ran with her into the ice cold water. They rushed out of the lake almost as quickly as they'd entered. Afterwards, wrapped in warm quilts, they sat as close as possible to the fire while Leon combed the tangles out of Gisela's long blonde hair.

Gisela leaned close to whisper, "Like living in teepee now."

The day the new couple returned home, Leon confronted Nathan. "Where did you get that white teepee?"

"Well, did you like it?"

"Of course, it was perfect--like a dream. But where did it come from?"

"We made it."

"Come on! It was a perfect Shawnee teepee. You can't make something like that."

"Aunt Mag once told me she'd seen the remains of one in Mr. Tinkerslea's wares. He bought it from an old Indian who was moving and couldn't take it with him. I was supposed to tell you about it, but I forgot until I needed to plan your honeymoon. The girls at Mama's boutique got all excited about making a honey-moon destination for you and Gisela. They used that old teepee for their pattern. We couldn't get skins, but they found some old oiled canvas in the rafters at The Mercantile that would do. They worked on it for hours. When they finished it, somehow Marcus and I figured out how to set it up with those old poles. It was quite a challenge."

"But this must've been expensive in the long run."

"Don't worry about that. Mr. Les was glad to get rid of that old canvas so he almost gave it away."

"What will happen to it now?"

"That's up to you. It's yours. It's not going anywhere." He nudged Leon in the ribs. "Why not visit your teepee again some-time soon...with your wife?"

Nathan ducked as Leon lunged for him.

CHAPTER 47

ith all the changes and developments in Springdale and the large Fresh Meadows family, the Norcutts' Christmas Open House had become the main event of the holiday season. A huge decorated tree stood in the parlor waiting for visitors from all over the area.

"This is getting out of hand," Adam whispered to Clarissa as they welcomed their long line of guests. "We may have to start sending invitations to a select guest list."

"Not in my lifetime, Adam. This is a big event for our family as well as our town. Since you're now our Mayor, it's even more important for us to host our annual party."

"But how can I possibly supply wassail for an entire town?"

"I'm sure you'll find a way. Why not ask Dr. Hugh to help? Doesn't he still have access to a big wine cellar in Lexington?"

"Yes, he probably does. But I doubt there's a locomotive capable of hauling all the liquor we'll need if this event gets much bigger."

"Need I say, God will provide? He's done it before."

Adam squeezed her hand as they welcomed their next group of friends.

Among their guests were two who'd never attended the event before, certainly not together. Wearing a new dress Gisela made for her at the Ladies' Fashion Boutique, Aunt Mag was on the arm of a well-attired Mr. Tinkerslea.

After greeting their hosts, Aunt Mag whispered in Clarissa's ear. "Mr. Tinkerslea has asked for my hand in marriage and I have accepted."

Clarissa, at first speechless, embraced her long time friend in a warm hug and pulled her away from the receiving line. They whispered together while the Tinker Man stood to the side, glowing.

"Thank you, Miss Clarissa," said Aunt Mag. "I'm so happy. So far, the only person opposed to my marriage to this wonderful gentleman is Miss Pru."

"Don't worry, she frets over everything. She's our local fly in the ointment."

"I've told Mr. Tinkerslea he'll have to get rid of most of those awful odds and ends he used to sell. But only after I go through them." The women wept with giggles. "But we've also talked about starting a shop together. He can sell his treasures and I can sell my cookies."

When Adam came over and found out what was going on, he shook hands with the happy couple. Later that afternoon, he quieted the crowded drawing room. Standing with the bride and groom, he announced their engagement news to everyone. After the applause died down, Clarissa made an announcement of her own.

"Ladies, don't you agree we should have a Pounding for Aunt Mag before her wedding? We don't know their wedding date yet, but we want this lady to have plenty of supplies for baking those famous cookies of hers. And now she'll be cooking for a husband."

"He sure loves to eat," said Aunt Mag when everyone applauded again.

Clarissa claimed Christmas Day with her family as her favorite day of the year. She always hurried to dress early so she could be the first one downstairs. This Christmas morning was no different.

"Hurry, Adam!" She shook his shoulder still buried under their down comforter. "The twins will be up as soon as it gets light. We won't be able to contain them, so you'd better get dressed. Right now."

"Yes'um." Adam yawned and went over to light the fire he'd laid in the stove the night before. Standing in front of the fire, he lingered to warm his hands.

"Adam! Stop that! Get ready!"

Clarissa sat at her dressing table and brushed out her long auburn hair. A few strands of silver now grew along her widow's peak. Quickly she turned her hair into a long French Braid, and tied it off with a bright red ribbon.

"I already hear Magnolia rattling around out in the kitchen, so I'm going over to help her. We'll need lots of tea and hot chocolate. She baked your favorite scones for breakfast. So hurry, and try to be quiet."

"Lead the charge, my dear."

When the Norcutt family opened their gifts, the twins were immediately enthralled with a large set of building blocks hand-made by Adam with Willy's help. Nathan provided pecans, shelled and roasted in salt and butter.

"Why, these are wonderful, son. When did you learn to do this?" asked Clarissa, reaching for another roasted pecan.

"Magnolia was my supervisor. Honestly, the hardest part was shelling those nuts. I hope it was all worth it!"

Polly and Hugh gave the most exciting gift of the morning to Clarissa and Adam. They handed them a heavy ivory envelope with a rich red wax seal. Inside was a note:

Dear Grandmother and Grandfather Norcutt,

I am coming for an extended visit next June or July.
I can't wait to meet you.

Love, Baby Perry

"What a gift!" said Adam, as he and Clarissa hugged the happy parents-to-be.

"Sorry we can't tell you if your long term guest is a boy or a girl," said Dr. Hugh.

"A healthy grandbaby is who we'll hope and pray for," said Adam.

Adam gave Clarissa a new bottle of Fresh Meadows perfume.

"But how did you find this, Adam?" she asked. "Now that Father's drug store is closed, I didn't think it was available."

"I shared my dilemma with Lester Lewis and now The Springdale Mercantile will stock this perfume."

After all the family gifts were exchanged, those who kept Fresh Meadows Farm up and running were invited in for their gifts and bonuses.

With a little help from Aunt Mag, Gisela baked traditional German Christmas cookies for everyone. She and Leon gave Miss Clarissa one of Blue Lark's turquoise stones on a chain. Leon gave Adam an old, but very sharp, Shawnee knife he discovered in Mr. Tinkerslea's storehouse. Because the Jonas negative balance had grown at The Mercantile during the renovations of Gisela's farm, the Norcutts paid off some of Leon's balance at the Mercantile.

The last gift handed out was a small box for Gisela. When she tore off the wrappings, she found a box of sugar cubes.

"I like, thank you." But she looked up at Leon with questions in her eyes.

"Isn't that enough?" asked Adam.

Gisela, still puzzled, nodded her agreement. "Yes, Herr Doctor, of course it is."

"Save a couple of cubes, but look outside for someone who will eat the rest."

She ran out the front door to find her gift. Tied to the veranda railing stood a perfectly groomed Herr Schwarz.

"Why he here? I already give him sugar cube today, Herr Doctor."

"He's yours now," said Adam. "We've noticed the close bond you have with this rambunctious gelding. If you can gentle him, we want you to have him. Merry Christmas!"

"Did you know?" Gisela confronted Leon.

"Sort of, because I had to prepare a stall for him at New Creek."

"So I keep?"

"Of course, he's yours," said Adam. "But it may take some time for Miner Boy to share his limelight."

As Gisela enjoyed her gift, Adam leaned in to speak quietly to Leon. "I'd like for you to give an idea of mine some thought. Gisela is so good with horses, as you are. Perhaps someday we should join efforts between Fresh Meadows and New Creek? We could raise some mighty good horseflesh together. What do you say to that idea?"

"I'm speechless, Mr. Doctor."

"We could..."

Unannounced, Sunny, wild-eyed, rushed out onto the veranda.

"Mr. Doctor, come quick! Papa! Come see what my Girlie did! She's such a bad kitty!"

"Sunny? What's happened?" Gisela rushed to her aid.

"Come see! I'll show you. I'm sorry she's made such a mess."

Sunny pulled on Adam's sleeve. Clarissa followed along to see what disaster had happened. Sobbing, the tearful little girl stopped them in front of Adam's East Windows.

"Sunny, it looks like all's well out in my meadows. Why are you so upset?" asked Adam.

"But lookie here, Mr. Doctor!" She pulled him around to face his favorite armchair. "My Girlie made a really bad mess. I'm so sorry. I'll clean up."

Reclining regally in Adam's armchair lay a triumphant Girlie with her first batch of kittens.

Everyone looked at one another and suppressed their laughter. Clarissa leaned down to hug the sobbing child.

"Sunny, everything is just fine. You have nothing to worry about. You should be very proud of Girlie. She just picked a very safe, quiet place on Christmas Day to have her babies."

"So those wiggly things are Girlie's? Her very own babies?"

"Yes, Sunny, and now we must take good care of them and keep them safe," said Adam. Looking over Sunny's curls at Clarissa, he raised an eyebrow and mouthed, "This cat has ruined my chair!"

"Adam, all's well. We've just welcomed our newest in need of a safe place to live."

Adam smiled down at Sunny. "Fresh Meadows Farm has always been a safe place."

BE KIND

"Always try to be kind to each other,
and to everyone else."

I Thessalonians 5:15

DISCUSSION QUESTIONS

1. What motivates Leon to rescue a strange waif?

2. Why does Gisela trust Leon?

3. What are Adam and Clarissa's initial responses to Gisela? Why?

4. Why does Gisela grieve when she sees the abandoned Featherson farm?

5. Should Adele have discussed Hugh's parentage with him?

6. What does Adele's secret stir up in Adam?

7. Are family secrets ever beneficial? If so, when?

8. Name the 'lost' characters rescued in this story, and in the entire Springdale Series.

9. Who dies in *Have Mercy!*?

10. Which people from the past continue to impact the characters' well-being?

11. Do our current racial and social issues appear in this story?

12. With whom do you identify in *Have Mercy!*?

13. What would you change in *Have Mercy!*?

14. What is theme of each book in the *Springdale Series*?

SPRITZGEBAECK

Traditional German Cookie Recipe

2/3 C Real Butter
1/2 C Sugar
3/4 C Flour
1/2 C Almonds -crushed very fine.
1 tsp Baking Powder
1 tsp Vanilla
1 Egg

Directions:

1.) Mix butter, sugar, egg, and vanilla together until creamed together well.
2.) Add flour, baking powder, and almonds. Mix well.
3.) Leave dough covered 1/2 hour in refrigerator.
4.) Put chilled dough into cookie press.
5.) Squeeze out amount needed to form cookies in shape you wish.
6.) Bake 12 minutes at 325 degrees.

Recipe thanks to Alexandra Depuhl, my dear friend in Germany,.

"HE GIVETH MORE GRACE"

He giveth more grace when the burdens grow greater,
He sendeth more strength when the labors increase,
To added affliction, He addeth His mercy,
To multiplied trials, His multiplied peace.

His love has no limit; His grace has no measure,
His power has no boundary known unto men,
For out of His infinite riches in Jesus,
He giveth and giveth and giveth again.

When we have exhausted our store of endurance,
When our strength has failed ere the day is half-done,
When we reach the end of our hoarded resources,
Our Father's full giving is only begun.

Annie Johnson Flint 1866-1932

(Perhaps this was one of Clarissa's favorite hymns?)

ACKNOWLEDGMENTS

I owe many thanks to my patient daughters,
Brenda Morris, Barbara Nelson, Mary McKee.
To partners Kathy Tolan, Charlynn Johns, Alexandra Depuhl.
To my many encouraging friends.
I'm blessed that each of you joined me
throughout the saga of *The Springdale Series*.

Martha B. Hook, MA is a fourth-generation Texan. She has three daughters, twelve grandchildren, and one great-grandson. She lives in Tyler, TX.

Order books through XulonPress, Amazon.com, or Barnes and Noble.

CPSIA information can be obtained
at www.ICGtesting.com
Printed in the USA
BVHW030541060820
585667BV00001B/26